GaiaSymphony:

Glass Shadow

Written By: Riley Howard

Phase 1 Book 1

Table of Contents

Prologue 3

The Beckoning 6

Maelstrom 9

The Great Machine 14

The Lone Protector 20

The Secrets of the Pillars 28

A Reason to Dream 35

A Walk In My Mind 47

The Things We Hide 56

Will You Answer the Call? 65

Blind Goddess 70

Setting Out 72

First Contact 79

The Parting 90

Hell's Gate 99

The Other Side of Solace 106

Glaive 115

Her Secrets 122

Beneath the Surface 124

The Otherworlder 132

Missing Rendezvous 143

Fate Realigned 149

Connection Established 151

Prologue

This city had always been bustling. It was a marvel of technological genius upheld by the team at DRAIDA Corp. Thanks to them, most of the city was entirely automated. The machines that aided this pursuit were able to increase the quality of life for almost every citizen who could afford the luxury. The innermost communities had always been kept pristine to perpetuate a positive image on their Overseers. As one could imagine, these communities were generally inhabited by the folks on the wealthier side. The city's name, Malvora. Governed by the word of Etharrow Khyron and Lunalia Lysithea, all was meant to be kept in smooth working order.

A problem had arisen, however. Many citizens believed that the two Overseers had grown complacent in their duties, speculating that organized crime had been allowed to flourish under their covert order. The people saw this as a threat to their way of life and sought to have them voted out, come the next election. The two had difficulties conjuring up a plan to save face, due to the increased negativity expressed by the expanding population of Malvora. The only groups willing to aid in the endeavor were the already known syndicates, whom the people feared. Overseers Khyron and Lysithea turned their attention to a small group of scientists from Bios- Alpha Laboratories Theta sector. Under the order of the Overseers, the scientists were enlisted into producing a solvable threat that would make Khyron and Lysithea look like heroes. The answer to this request was the creation of a race of beings known as the Vyrida. These beings were conceived for the sole purpose of wreaking havoc on the unsuspecting city. Bios-Alpha had indicated to the Overseers that the Vyridia could be shut down if things became too much to handle. The Overseers, seeing the potential this plan had, agreed to all sentiments.

The test did not go according to plan however when the scientists unleashed the Vyridia into the world, they didn't wreak any aforementioned havoc. Instead, they greeted their new surroundings with profound curiosity. While many of them were timid as newborn deer, others quickly adapted to life out in Malvora. The citizens of Malvora were puzzled at the sudden appearance of these strange entities and began voicing their concerns. Many people had made reports of seeing wings on the backs of these creatures, phasing in and out of reality. Most claims were dismissed as crackpot theories, but as the number of incidents grew, it became difficult to bolster this belief.

The Overseers saw this opportunity to mount a societal attack on the beings, scapegoating them as the catalyst to the descent of the city. Malvora fell into divided chaos. This panned out well for Khyron and Lysithea who had regained the popular vote. Since Vyridian rights hadn't been established, there were none to abolish. The defenseless, wide-eyed race had come under fire. Many were killed by Malvoran citizens, as no constitution sat in place to protect them. Their executions were often encouraged, even. Many Vyridia ended up in the slums in the outer communities of the city, yet even there, their reception was not warm. Small resistance groups began popping up, threatening the operations of the Overseers. Most of these factions were stamped out by the Overseers Military police force known as 'The Phantom Ravens'. Few had survived the onslaught but pushed forward in their fight for emancipation. As the years dragged on, one faction would rise above the hatred and bring the Overseers reign of tyranny to a grinding halt. The group known as Eclypse had been working with the now-defected Bios- Alpha in a ploy to remove the Overseers from power. The leader of Eclypse, a sprightly Vyridia by the name of Solsta Goodwill, took to the streets of Malvora with his troupe and initiated violent acts on the city and its people. Many other Vyridia and the Malvoran people who sympathized with them saw this as an act of justice and too joined in on the vagrant activity. These expressions had drawn out a long-held secret, kept by the Overseers. The truth that they had been puppeteered by a higher governing force the entire time. Eclypse had come face to face with Aios Circaea, a powerful being known as a Vaskyr, who much like the Vyridia possessed a pair of wings that too would phase in and out of sight. Aios had revealed the nature of the existence of the Vyridia. It turned out that early Vyridia were a product of reproduction between a Vaskyr and a Malvoran. This hybrid was seen as an impurity by the Vaskyr and Aios Circaea was sent to eradicate it. The battle between Eclypse and Aios Circaea resulted in the deaths of both Circaea and Solsta Goodwill.

Before their departure, Eclypse, alongside numerous Bios-Alpha team members, reveal another secret that had been squirreled away by the former Overseers.

That oxygen levels on the planet had been depleting at a rapid pace. This phenomenon became known as 'The Shift' and had many people on edge about future prospects for the city and planet.

As Eclypse dissolved and faded into obscurity, many wondered what came next. They all feared they were too blind to see what lied in store.

Chapter 1- The Beckoning

Llaric Ephyon- 35

It was the slowest demise we could have ever faced. Slow, yet unpreventable. Excruciating with no end in sight. There was nothing we could do. After the government fell, we were left to fend for ourselves. The place I called home was a couple of hours out of Malvora, a once-great city teeming with the most awe-inspiring technological advancements. It fell to the uprising of Eclipse, a revolutionary group of beings known as the Vyridia and those that sympathized with them. The Overseers that once ruled the city despised them. I never really paid any mind or fell to the fear that they spoon-fed us. I left the city with my daughter, Ophelia when the riots started. I sought refuge at an outpost west of the city. When I got there, the whole place was in disarray. Blood had stained almost every corner. I set to work fixing it up so that my daughter could grow up peacefully away from the chaos of Malvora. However, life out here wasn't easy. Access to food was scarce unless we braved the gauntlet of the city. To make matters worse, every day, every waking second was spent tending to them. The greatest fear one could face in these times is the death of their Anchor. Plants stored in specialized capsules called 'Esperata', were the key to our continuation. After the oxygen started disappearing from the very space around us in an anomaly we all knew as 'The Shift', the governments of our world sanctioned the last remaining plants to their citizens. A hefty fee was implied for the replacement of a lost or dead Anchor, and soon the matters became dire, as the very gardens in the soil began to die. The earth beneath, which once sustained the abundant life force, grew sterile and eventually became a barren wasteland. A desolate reminder of our fate, fast- encroaching. I knew that this crutch couldn't support us for much longer. The early days of the Shift were much more civil. Life went on rather normally. People were always willing to help out one another. That was of course until the government could no longer provide Anchors. They all turned on one another like animals. Greed overtook sensibility as the whole world fell into depravity. While everyone was feeding the frenzy that became them, I sought answers. I sought a way out of this living hell. The nightmares began almost as soon as I lost her. My daughter, Ophelia.

    I awoke one morning in our pod and found that she had disappeared. The entire place was upheaved, a small window on the side of the property was broken and copious amounts of blood led back to it from her room. I immediately assumed the worst. However, when I bolted outside to find out which way the blood trail went, I was greeted with a rather mysterious predicament. There was no blood to be found. Completely clean. I had run back inside to see if I could find any evidence of someone being in the house. I went to her room and noticed her Anchor still in its Esperata. I spent months searching but to no avail. I trusted no one as most of the world had seemingly gone feral. I often found myself fighting off or hiding from raiders that scoped the lands in search of more Anchors. I had begged whatever gods would listen, to bring her back to me but deep in my mind, I knew I wouldn't like their response if I could ever hear one.
5 months in I knew that no hope remained. No one could survive the conditions for more than a few days without an Anchor, let alone 5 months. She was 5 years old. I had failed her. The only thing I had left.
 Something kept nagging me to find answers to our downfall as a species. I knew that the loss and grievance would never truly disappear, but I had to move my focus back to staunching the Shift.
Eventually, I had to let go. The nightmares were getting worse and so was my situation. I couldn't rest on my Sorrow any longer. I had

little solace and nothing to go on so I set to work analyzing my nightmares. Seeing if there was anything they could tell me. They were always very similar. It was a long shot, this I knew, starting with anything was better than standing on nothing. I pulled from the far recesses of my memory the image of a dark, lumbering creature. Its eyes were a piercing white color, surrounded by rotting flesh and exposed bone.

I would see it in every one of these terror- riddled phantasmagoria, just... staring. Endless, rolling whispers emanated from its body. Countless voices, yet not one coherent. I would just stare back, paralyzed... Catatonic. Still. Then I would awake in the dead of night with one final whisper chasing me out of my unconscious mind. This one was always different, because I could understand it, and without fail, every night as I was jolted from slumber, I'd hear the words,

"Without Yggdrasil, we fall".

Then. Silence.

Chapter 2- Maelstrom

Zephyr Apherius- 24

     Without an anchor, I have been scouring the desolation for as long as I can remember. I had previously established a connection with a small collection of revolutionaries who safe-housed hundreds of oxygen tanks. They called themselves 'Maelstrom'. I thought it was corny, but everyone else seemed to find a sense of purpose in the name, so I kept my thoughts on it to myself. Who was I to take that away from them? For a while, it was comforting to be sitting on such an abundance of oxygen. The downside, however, was that, unlike the Anchors, the tanks could not provide a perpetual exchange of gasses. Soon we found ourselves needing more. Fights began erupting among us on how to divvy up the precious commodity. Many among us believed that the government was holding out on oxygen distribution in an attempt to establish a market later on for the extremely desperate. We all had concluded that it had to be taken if it wasn't offered. Living in the wastes was harsh. Sustenance was heavily scarce, water levels were depleting and the reserves that did exist were heavily guarded. I chuckled to myself.
If only my father could see me. A common thief among thieves. How noble we'd all become. I am grateful to him though. I would have hated to see him in the position I'm in now. The Anchor he saved my life with was long gone. I was so stupid. I was so stupid to think that I could bring the gardens back. Thinking we had a chance. I knew it was a futile attempt, yet I still explored the wastes in search of blessed, fertile soil. Growing up, I always sought to help the people out of this calamity. Bring them solace with my bountiful gardens. I never wanted to be the one stealing oxygen from them. I wasn't exactly the beacon of hope that I had

wanted to grow into, but I wasn't about to stop trying. The only way I could see my dream come to fruition, was to survive.
If a couple of people had to fall to cater to the needs of the many, then that was the way it had to be. As unfortunate as it was, I had no other choice. If I wasn't moving forward every day, then I might as well have died with my father when I was a little girl.

      Kash, one of my fellow revolutionaries, was loading tanks into the back of our truck. I approached and began handing them to him. As he clambered onto the tailgate he let out a long sigh.
 "What?", I asked with a small laugh.
 "Just the thought of fighting something that is well beyond us, day by day kind of defeats the purpose of hope, don't you think?"
 "That glass is still half-empty, hey?" I replied
 "That glass is empty and turned upside down, Zeph".
I knew morale around the Maelstrom camp was dwindling. The daily scavenge was wearing on some folks. Kash always tried to keep his spirits high for everyone else's sake, but I could see the toll that the monotony was taking on him, and who could blame him? I felt the same. If only I could bring them a continuous source of oxygen, at the very least, we could abolish our scavenging runs. I knew, however, that if I was going to find any semblance of fertile soil, I'd have to go beyond the boundary line. Doing that almost ensured death. I couldn't carry enough of the tanks with me to survive a trip that long. Bringing the truck out was too risky as we could be apprehended by raiders or get the vehicle stuck at the bottom of the canyon. I had often overlooked it seeing if there were any remaining green patches. I saw nothing but the bleak sands below. I'd have to go farther than I could see.
 Kash and I finished loading the last of the tanks into the truck. I closed the tailgate, and the sound of it seemed to perk everyone up.
Kash spoke out to them.
 "Katya, it's time to go.", he stated.

Katya, who was scribbling some notes onto a piece of yellowed paper, responded with her eyes still glued to the paper.
 "Sounds good. Just taking some notes on areas we haven't charted yet."
Katya was always ready to go. There were often times that I felt her gung- ho attitude was the only thing keeping our collective sanity in check. Even on the brink of disaster, she was always the one to get us through it. She had an odd obsession with cartography and lucky for the rest of us it gave us a pretty good idea of our surroundings.
 Katya pushed her jet black bangs out of her face and looked up at us. Her blue eyes almost glowed in the settling dusk. A voice rang out from the left of me.
 "I'm synched with your GPS and radar."
The voice was that of Valian Sorik. He was always rather serious but always had our best interests at heart. It was rare that he would join us on our ventures. He often opted to stay back at base and keep an eye on things. He would also keep an eye on us while we were away via satellite transmissions. Comms, radars, and GPS were all overseen by him. He could see threats approaching long before we could, so having him on the other end of the comms was always a comfort. It was all routine for me at this point. Without a thought, I hopped into the passenger seat. Katya elected to ride in the bed of the truck as she often did when she was scouting the land. We had even left a space free of tanks in the back so she could sit. I was always baffled that she could take such legible notes while her papers blew violently in the wind, we knew she wouldn't have it any other way. The headlights of our truck cut through the fast-approaching darkness as the sun began to disappear behind the horizon. The remaining natural light trading off of the grains of sand was picturesque. As our tires ran through, the light on that sand faded with the day.

 The ride was rather silent as Kash had to keep an ear out for Valian's directions. Most of the noise in the cab was just Kash confirming those directions until we came to the same familiar cold-looking wall. It was here that we would conduct our heist. We had done this countless times already with little resistance. I had recently developed a feeling of uncertainty about this place. Surely the governing forces would have noticed a drop in their supply by now. I often wished we had more resources, and more people to do this job. Perhaps it was just a futile effort to set my mind at ease. I knew full well that people in the wastes were few and far between, and the ones that did exist were dangerous raiders. I felt a breeze on my face that dragged me back to reality and I noticed that Kash was already out of the truck. He had backed into an under-crop to keep out of sight. I hopped out and quietly helped them unload tanks. Katya scoured her notes for the next scheduled guard round. According to them, we had about an hour before we had to start worrying about packing up. We had implemented an efficient system that would ensure the maelstrom receives the most oxygen all the while keeping losses to an absolute minimum. It was agreed upon that whoever was filling the tanks would stay behind as a distraction if the group was apprehended so that the other two had a chance to get away. No one was appointed to this position. We all took turns. One of us would remain at the truck and load in the full tanks while the other ran back and forth between the two. The work was tedious but needed to be done. Our survival was at stake. On this particular trip, I was appointed as a runner while Katya stayed behind and Kash filled the tanks. We had communications with Valian who was able to see oncoming entities through radar. It was a simple and effective plan. Yet I still felt uneasy a lot of the time. What if the guards change their routes? What if there is an ambush staged for us? There could be thousands of guards inside. We had set to work with the utmost haste. Kash and I each ran two empty tanks to the oxygen line. Kash began by shutting off the line and cutting into it. It was imperative that we replaced the piping after as well so as not to arouse more suspicion. I began running back to the truck. Katya already had a substantial number of tanks unloaded. I

grabbed two more and began running them back to Kash. I heard Valian over our comms saying he was hearing something.
I radioed back to ask him what direction it was coming from. He responded quietly saying that he heard something by our base, not by us. Then his comms went dark. I stopped in place and attempted to re-establish the connection. There was nothing but static over the radio waves. I rushed the two tanks I was carrying over to Kash who had also stopped. He turned to look at me, and for the first time in months, I saw worry painted across his face.

Chapter 3- The Great Machine

Llaric Ephyon- 35

    Everything was a mess. An endless sea of paper, with meaningless text, jotted haphazardly on most of it. Anything not covered in words was etched with scribbles of things that I had seen both within my dreams and outside of them. A cacophony of disorganized information. I had to see if any of it tied together. I even had hopes that Ophelia could bring me an answer. I wouldn't know unless I began piecing all of my information together. I worked tirelessly most days that I'd forget to eat. Not that food was in great abundance anyway. I honestly looked at my obsession as a gift. I was conserving my resources as analytics consumed me. I knew I couldn't quit until I found a way to staunch the bleeding of this dying world. I had no idea if I was heading in the right direction or not, but something in the back of my mind kept nagging me to look into this creature that I kept seeing in my dreams. It was almost as if it portrayed the rot that this world had succumbed to. I was beginning to lose sleep. It was in my mind that every second wasted was a thunderous boom on the doomsday clock. I needed answers. What was Yggdrasil? The creature kept repeating that word. Over and over it was driving me insane. The sleep depravity that I garnered from these roundabout questions brought me to the point of hallucination.

The veil between reality and the dream plane began thinning as I walked the border between them. I began seeing the creature in my home. Spying from every dark corner... and the rifts. Oh god, the rifts.

I tried my damndest to ignore them when they came, but sometimes I couldn't help myself. Through them, I would see depictions of horrific calamity, hordes of beings erased from existence. I saw the inception of a great construct in the depths of space. Whoever was building it, was utilizing foundation blocks I had never seen the likes of. Materials free-floating around the structure ominously. It looked like... a hotel? I couldn't analyze it further. The rifts came and went as they pleased just like my decaying sanity. After remaining awake for the better part of two weeks. I had decided that I was just spinning my tires and getting nowhere. I wanted the rifts to stop and most importantly, I wanted that... thing out of my house. I staggered off to my bedroom and crashed as soon as my head hit the pillow.

     I was awoken by an earth-shattering boom. A green flash of light soared over my still-closed eyes. This invasion of light caused me to shoot up, completely awake. I noticed one of the lights outside had turned on by itself. This was anomalous to me, as all the lights on my property worked on a grid. None of them were to be operating independently unless they were switched on manually. I pondered what could have caused this odd string of events.

My thoughts were interrupted by yet another light switching on. Then, I saw movement. It was somewhat distant but I could tell that whatever it was, it was moving closer. At first, my thoughts leaned to the prospect of raiders, but it was rare to see them this far out unless they possessed Anchors.

I then began to wonder if it was Ophelia coming home to me. All my inklings were dismissed after I saw the object grow nearer, however. It appeared to be a giant machine that had taken on a humanoid shape. Bladed protrusions extended from its back and a faint orange color glowed from its eyes. It floated silently over the sand and directly towards my pod. I noticed it stop and raise its hand towards another light. This light, as if being controlled by the being, turned on. The machine then turned and slowly began floating to other lights around the property. Naturally, I was frozen in terror.

What the hell was it? It was massive. Something like that moving as silently as it was, was haunting. It was clearly scanning for something, and I was hoping to the gods that it wasn't me. I watched every millimeter of movement the great machine made. It looked highly advanced, and I couldn't pinpoint who might have manufactured it.

It looked too high-tech to be anything local. It seemed even beyond the machines constructed by the prolific DRAIDA corporation. A group whose very name has spurned fantasies of it existing in other planes of reality. Mere stories. However, when a group is widely known for huge leaps in technological science, it's hard not to build conspiracies. Even my belief was shaken after seeing this monolithic creature.

It continued around the property, turning on every light it found and it was growing closer. All I could hear were my staggered breaths as I tried to force myself to keep them quiet. I could feel my lungs screaming for a steady stream of oxygen. I took in a deep breath and as if it were a beacon, the creature snapped its head in my direction. I ducked in cover under my window as the deep, orange glow of its eyes grew more intense. It knew I was here. Oddly enough, it didn't approach my window, even though the curtains were drawn widely. Instead, I noticed the orange lights disappear completely.

I slowly poked my head over the crest of the window sill and frantically looked around. It was gone. I saw no traces of it. I did unfortunately hear it. A sound from outside my room echoed through like death bells. The knob of my front door was rattling. I took the largest breath I could muster and climbed into my closet. I quietly shut the door and peeked out from the slats. I was convinced the being could hear my increasing heart rate as panic further set in. Yet still, I remained silent.

Then I heard it. the slow, familiar creak of my front door. I heard very faint whirring sounds. It sounded like some sort of propulsion device. A bright streak illuminated a portion of carpet in my room from under the door. I could only assume the being flipped the switch to the light in the hallway. I had so many thoughts racing in my head that I couldn't formulate a plan. I remained still as stone and awaited my fate. A shadow made itself present under my door. I closed my eyes. I let the darkness consume my vision. To my surprise, a voice seemed to reverberate in my head, leaving dancing colors on my eyelids with every syllable.

"Have no fear, truth- seeker. I am called Valiance, and I am here solely to provide you with the answers you've sought after. Step out so that I might look upon you. Have no fear, void- walker. I am but a light down the correct path. All will be revealed to you."

I felt comforted by these words. I knew I was being coaxed out of my hiding place, but then again was it really a hiding place? There's no doubt in my mind that this being knew exactly where I was. I couldn't say what compelled me to exit the closet and approach the handle of my bedroom door, but before I knew it my hand was on it. Turning. Opening. The goliath machine was right on the other side. I looked up and met its gaze. Its eyes grew ever brighter until they blinded me and then... once again I was unconscious.

It seemed akin to an enlightening nightmare. The kind you have that scares you initially but educates you in the end. My mind was scattered. I didn't know if it was all a dream or if I hadn't slept at all. The lines between reality and those of other planes were still blurred. Either way, through this event I had learned something. A greater calling did indeed await me, and I had arrived at new conclusions. Avenues that I didn't even seem to know of, were now illuminated. It was my belief that 'Yggdrasil' was a spiritual connection to all things. Branches connecting our reality to others. I had also been studying my Anchor and Esperata. The newfound ideas spread through my head like wildfire. The roots of these anchors would work similarly to the proverbial branches of Yggdrasil.

I realized that I was looking at it all wrong. Sleeping as often as I could to study the creature of my nightmares was further burying me in this singular reality. If I could reach out to others, perhaps there would be a chance on which I could hinge the survival of my people.

Wait. Was I a lunatic? I had never had such thoughts cross my mind. Conspiracies and folklore? Perhaps I was just growing desperate. I reminded myself that I should keep an open mind. Perhaps some paths were available that were just never explored. Besides, I had witnessed many strange things. A lot of which had no explanation.

No. I had to push forward. I had to try anything as it came to my mind. They always say quality over quantity when it comes to ideas, but surely an endless quantity is sure to procure some quality results.

I decided to continue with my plan. Sleep deprivation would connect me to these other realities. The rifts I had previously tried to ignore with my incessant scribbling would provide the answers I need. It was odd. The air around me felt lighter. Breathing seemed easier. Had I been working in a panic this whole time? Had I truly never stopped to breathe and just take a step back?

    All the building blocks were laid before me, I was just too scrambled to see them. One thing still remained unanswered at the back of my mind... That machine I saw last night.

    I stepped outside to see if there were any traces of its presence and immediately I had my final question answered. All of the lights that it had turned on were still glowing brightly in the mid-day sun. As I brought my gaze down to the left I had also noticed a large collection of metal and wires all neatly organized down to the smallest parts. I had no idea how this large supply of products got here. As I stared at it, however, I was stricken with a violent headache. Flashes of my basement were presenting themselves to me and within it, another large machine. This machine was nothing like the one in my yard last night. This one was stationary and seemingly had no function.

My headache ceased and I was re-grounded. I was torn between feelings of psychosis and revelation. This was tearing my sanity apart like thin parchment, but I couldn't let it get the best of me. All I had to do to stave it off was to keep focused on a singular thing. I told myself to forget the collection of metal outside my pod for now and come back to it when I have seen what I need to.

I sat at my kitchen table with my Anchor in front of me. I attempted to use it as a vessel to keep my mind awake. I aimed to separate my mind from my body resulting in a perpetual state of wakefulness, mentally. My body, devoid of its consciousness, would be my tether to reality. With this tether, I could apply reality to the dream-like state I was in, subsequently rendering both as a singular existence. I was hoping this plan could allow me to traverse realities using the rifts I had experienced earlier. It all seemed perfectly in order. As the first rift opened, I knew I had gotten something right. I was face to face with other beings. I greeted them with a burning excitement. A greeting that was not reciprocated. It was as if they weren't aware of my existence. I felt as though I was a silent spectator in their world, sitting alongside them in a meeting of higher matters. I was intrigued by these new beings. They called themselves 'The Pillars of Light'.

Chapter 4- The Lone Protector

Valian Sorik- 29

      I had cut the comms. I was certain my Maelstrom brethren would fare just fine for a brief period. I had heard a couple of voices nearby and could tell by the varying tones that they were raiders. Damn scavengers were high as hell on something. Lucky for me, they didn't exactly take the stealthy approach. I stifled any light source I could and scoured the area outside of the base to see just how close the scumbags were. It took me all of ten seconds to spot a lit cigarette floating ominously in the darkness. I quietly snuck back into my makeshift office and grabbed my trusty shotgun. I wasn't about to start firing into the wind though. I knew that even as high and stupid as these guys were, they'd overpower me with sheer numbers if I didn't scout the area properly. If I just stayed quiet, perhaps they might not even notice the base. They could slip by unharmed. I gazed down at my hands, second-guessing my choice of weapon. I quietly placed it on my chair, opting for my hunting knife instead. The voices drew closer and I could see through the fencing that they were passing by. I looked to be in the clear. As I was about to breathe a sigh of relief I realized that one was staggering behind. He got close enough to the fence that I could see just how wide his eyes were. This guy was tripping hard. There's no way he'd see me coming. Just as I thought I was home free, this bastard stopped to take a piss right through the fence. Disgusting. I couldn't go out there and just knife him. If I did that, the others might return and notice the blood. I had to get him inside quickly and silently if he happened to spot me. I stayed still in a crouching position by the door, ready to swing it open and grab him. He finished his business and babbled some incoherent nonsense before stumbling off after his buddies. I heard his body brush against the other side of the door as he passed. I had to remain vigilant. They could be back this way at any point. I elected to get back on comms and let everyone know they were on their own for the rest of the mission. After I was sure they had gone, I got up and plopped myself back in my chair, and flicked all my comms switches back on. As the static rang, I called out,

"Hey! You guys still alive? Sorry for the blackout. A group of raiders came by and pissed on the base."

Zephyr Apherius- 24

It was a relief to hear Valian. After he let us in on the situation, he elected to shut down comms for the rest of our mission to keep an eye on the raiders near our base. Katya hopped in the truck and monitored radar herself while I ran the remaining empty tanks to Kash.

"That was a close call with Valian, don't you think?", I asked as I got to him.

"It was too close of a call. I'm thinking one of us stays behind next time", he replied.

I nodded slightly shaken at the idea of raiders taking over our base.

I waited for Kash to fill the last two tanks before we made our final trip back to the truck. I heard the hiss of rushing air as he detached the last tank and snapped the line closed. He set to work repairing the line. It was always gratifying to see the finished product. It looked like it was never touched. We each heaved two tanks over our shoulders and made our way back towards the truck. As we began running up the last dune the beam of a flashlight appeared.

"Dammit!", I muttered angrily. Kash pulled me down into the sand on the right side of a wall opening. We could hear the shifting of the sand as footsteps grew closer. It appeared to be a guard. I knew our luck had to run out sometime but now of all times? Right when we had the last four tanks?! As he grew closer I heard him mumbling something. He was repeating the same thing over like a skipping record. When I could finally hear what it was that he was saying, a deep chill ran down my spine. As he passed I heard him say,

"Without Yggdrasil, we fall".

Why this spooked me, I don't know, but I had an overwhelming feeling of deja vu. I looked at Kash who kept his gaze fixed on the guard.

As the guard reached the other side of the opening in the wall he seemed to dissipate into thin air. The rambling voice stopped and so did the footsteps. His light faded into nothingness too. He was just gone before our very eyes. Kash and I looked at each other slowly. We were both in disbelief at what had just transpired. We made a break for the truck. We were both too frightened to look back. We just kept running full bore until we rendezvoused with Katya. We threw the last of the tanks in the back and hustled into the truck. I could hear Kash fumbling with the keys. I couldn't even bring myself to look. My eyes were glued to the darkness outside the windshield. Katya took immediate notice.

"What the hell's gotten into you two? Did you see something?"

Kash immediately shot a question her way.

"Did you pick up anything on the radar?"

"N-no, there was nothing", she stuttered. "What the hell happened out there?", she asked.

I told her we would discuss it after we got back to base and made sure Valian was alright.

It was strange, we had seen that guard many times during the day while tracking his patrol times. We never once thought to check the radar while observing. I was completely convinced that we had just witnessed a ghost. I was led to other thoughts. Perhaps the facility we had been taking oxygen from was empty. What if the facilitators of the oxygen had died off long ago? It made sense to me as our patterns were never picked up on. Stranger still was that we knew we made a dent in the oxygen levels within the structure, so why had no one looked into it? Besides the guard that came by about twenty minutes early, nothing else seemed out of routine. Furthermore, that guard turned out to be a ghost. A lone protector, not even aware of his own demise.

I knew we were both hoping that exhaustion had just gotten the better of us, but we were still rattled by the experience.

With fear, however, came curiosity. I had the urge to explore the building further. To see if anything still thrived within the walls. I kept the idea to myself until we debriefed back at base. As we rolled in, Valian was smoking just outside the door. He stood up to help unload the newly filled tanks.

"You're not looking too good, Zeph", he said with a cigarette still pursed in his lips.

"Her and Kash have been freaking out the whole ride home", Katya interjected.

Valian gave us both a strange look and chuckled lightly before saying,

"Did you see a ghost or something?"

His smile dropped as we both stared back at him with dead serious expressions. He beckoned us inside the base and sat us all down.

We had replenished 54 tanks. I was exhausted, but we still had to debrief any findings. I explained to Valian and Katya, the event that Kash and I had witnessed as best I could. I also brought up the idea that we plan a search into the building.

"That's not going to happen", Kash stated. "I can't hinge the life of my fellow Maelstrom on a hunch."

"Consider it a hunt for answers, Kash", I retorted. "If it turns out we've been sitting on an abandoned, untapped gold mine of oxygen this whole time, wouldn't you want to be closer to the source? It would mean the end of lugging these things around.", I added as I thumbed the giant stack of tanks behind me. "Think about it, if there is no living soul in that facility, it may even have a few Anchors laying about. We could move our operations there."

He looked at me as if I were stupid.

"Zephyr, you are basing this information off of something that we aren't even sure that we saw."

I responded yet again, slightly heated.

"Risks are all we have left! You want to continue this, day in and day out? Do you want to hang everything in your life on this reality? A reality where we have to STEAL air? AIR, Kash."

Katya pipped up and shared her piece on my statement.

"I know I'm sick of the daily grind. What's the point of all my documentation when I could die tomorrow? Or any of us for that matter?"

Kash swapped his gaze between Katya and me in disbelief. He finally looked over to Valian who smirked and shrugged.

"Can't argue with that, my man."

Kash remained silent. It was obvious that he didn't want to follow through with such a bare-bones operation, but I could see that even he knew we were exhausting our options. He looked down, likely weighing his options. After a brief spell of pondering he looked back up at us with a deep sigh.

"What's the plan?", he asked.

I felt the smile grow across my face. For the first time in forever, I felt a semblance of hope. There was a glimmer of a future for us. Fortified walls and limitless oxygen, with the chance to find Anchors. We would be set for the rest of our lives. I, of course, had no plan yet and agreed that we couldn't move forward without one, so I set to work. I enlisted the help of Katya as her cartography skills could come in handy. She also had a keen eye for detail. If there were any ways in that weren't the front door, she would already have tabs on them.

"There's no other way in".

I was in disbelief. Katya had found nothing in the way of secret entrances. Not a single design flaw, not even an air duct. I brought up the idea of sewer travel to which she launched a disgusted stare in my direction.

"Unfortunately and surprisingly, that is also not an option. I didn't notice any drainage pipes around the facility, nor any openings into the system. So if they have anything of the sort, it's all purely internal", Katya mentioned. "There is the possibility that they extended and hid the air duct entrances farther away from the facility. It would reduce the efficiency of airflow, but would ensure that no one can get in unless they use the main doors."
 It was quite an inconvenience. We had no idea how far out a duct could go and we couldn't afford to spend all day digging for them in the blazing hot sun. On top of that, we had the possibility of being spotted by raiders or potential Government officials. We concluded that the only answer was to sneak right in the front door. We had ample cover to hide behind, as hundreds of facility vehicles filled the parking lot to the front door. Unfortunately, there were no windows to peek through. We were hoping we could slip in undetected. I pondered the risks as I laid down for the night. My eyes grew heavy rather quickly. The strenuous day had finally caught up with me, as my cot slowly pulled me into the miasma of unconsciousness.

    Sleeping was always something I looked forward to. I was often greeted with tidbits of the old world I knew. Memories of my father and friends would play over and over like a home movie. It was the purest coping mechanism I could think of and often kept me going in the perilous conditions of the wasteland. Tonight, the memories of my Father and I walking through an old city reeled over my eyes. It was bustling with people.
 Talking, laughing, bartering. I felt pure ecstasy. Various markets lined the streets. The peacoats of passers-by billowed in the light breeze. Even the darkening rain clouds in the sky were welcomed with the warmest smile.
 Everything came over me as vividly as the day it happened. the cool air, the smell of cigarette smoke, and most of all the smiles of strangers as they went about their lives. I had such an overwhelming feeling of nostalgia. What was it even like to just

live? I don't remember. What I wouldn't have given to experience this again. I looked up at my father.

If only he knew how much I missed him. How much I wished I could turn back time and see his smile once again. He looked down at me with a sincere grin and placed his hand on my head. I suppose the perfection of that day couldn't be immortalized in my memory.

I remembered everything as clear as crystal, and I sure as hell didn't remember the heat ripples emanating off of the sidewalk. I didn't remember the shadows bleeding from the alleyways. Pulsating as if they were alive. Something was corrupting my dreams, and then I saw something out of place. A little girl with her back turned to me. Her right hand was being held by a man that I didn't recognize from that day. Her left hand grasped a string connected to a floating black balloon. As the people shuffled by, she remained still. I apprehensively approached, but she began moving forward. I quickened my pace to match theirs but I could not. It was futile. She disappeared into the crowd with the man I could only assume was her father. As she disappeared, so did the pulsing and the reaching shadows. I was puzzled. I distinctly remembered every event of this day. There was no little girl carrying a black balloon. I was curious as to why this anomaly allowed everything to go back to normal. Could it be that my sheer will prevented an unwanted nightmare? The air returned to its smoky aroma, and the people went about their day as if nothing had transpired. I was slightly shaken by the events that had unfolded. I had decided to remain vigilant for the remainder of the dream and see if I could pick out any other oddities. My father and I walked past a newspaper stand. The newspapers always had a distinct smell as we passed. I looked down expecting to see the familiar headline 'Tensions Mount As Atmosphere Breaks Down'. Instead, I was greeted with something far more sinister. A phrase that I had not heard since childhood. The phrase that I had been pondering since the day it first presented itself to me.

"WITHOUT YGGDRASIL WE FALL"

I coiled back in fear. The entities within my dreamscape took notice and all stopped to stare. The world stood still as it often did in my younger years. As I looked up towards the proprietor of the stand, I wasn't greeted by the smiling old man I was used to seeing, but instead by a gruesome monster. A hulking dark figure that looked to be rotting. Its eyes were glazed over, dead as the stillness around me. A strange smoke appeared to be emanating off of its carrion flesh. Its head snapped towards me and it slowly began opening its mouth. The sound that came from it could only be described as the blood curdling screams of the damned. I opened my mouth to scream in tandem, but no sound ever passed my lips. I knew right at that moment, there was no mistaking it. I knew exactly what I was looking at. The creature before me came to be known as the Umbra.

I coined this name due to the darker than black smoke that billowed from the creature's being, and also due to its hidden intentions. I had not seen it plague my dreams since the day my Father died.

Something ominous was on the horizon. Something that I thought was long dead.

Chapter 5- The Secrets of the Pillars

Llaric Ephyon- 35

The exchange was puzzling, to say the least. The three Pillars roamed about a grand hall conversing about the effects of a so-called 'Insidian'. From what I had gathered, the three had undertaken an oath to satiate the hunger of a fourth-dimensional being that far surpassed them in strength and knowledge. Two of them appeared to be in an argument about the best way to settle their contract with the god-like entity, while the third caught my attention. He was exclaiming remarks about the process of transcendence. While the others continued prattling on about a great war that devastated their people,
the third was offering up the suggestion to evolve and face Insidian. A message burned into my brain. An image of text that I had never seen before.

"The fierce one roams"

 A steady stream of new images flooded my mind. Pictures of a creature that walked endlessly, decimating everything in its path. I was immediately reminded of the dark creature that plagued my dreams. Endlessly stalking and destroying my very sanity. As they continued they discussed the fact that there was no tangible aspect of Insidian aside from a stone obelisk which the Pillars never mentioned the location of. It began to dawn on me that these Pillars may hold the answer to my dilemma as well. If I could learn the secrets to transcendence, and teach it to the residents on my planet, there would be no need for oxygen. There would be no need for the vessels that required it either. We wouldn't have to live in fear any longer. If the Pillars sought after transcendence, then surely others would too.

      Without thinking I called out to them. Nothing. I screamed relentlessly in hopes of grabbing their attention. My voice grew hoarse. A resounding pain throbbed in my head as the pressure built up within. Was there really no way to reach them?
 The pain began to plateau and the vision of the Pillars began to fade. I tried desperately to get their attention as they faded from existence, but it was futile. I grabbed my head in an attempt to soothe the pain. As the throbbing subsided, I looked up to find myself in an endless white room. I turned around to see that the Pillars were on some sort of screen, playing like a movie on a loop that I had been plucked from. I watched in deafening silence as they went about their arguments. This went on until I felt a light tug on my left sleeve. I looked over to my left and was taken aback. A little girl was standing next to me. Her hair was neatly pulled back with a headband. The index finger and thumb of her right hand were loosely gripping my sleeve while her left hand was adorned with a small white glove. In that hand was a string tied to a black balloon. The strangest part of this encounter was that the girl had no face. In the place where her face should have been, stood instead, a dark, light-sucking abyss, completely devoid of features. Yet with no discernable visage, I could still sense that she was staring blankly at the screen before us. Her breathing sounded labored and raspy. This breathing evolved into speech. Her voice sounded like nails on a chalkboard. It sent chills up my spine as she spoke, yet I remained unafraid.
      "Call his name", she said from the featureless void on her face.
I cocked my head to the side, confused at her request.
      "What's his name?", I replied.
 At that moment all fell truly silent once again. Her breathing stopped as did her words. Her head began turning slowly towards me.

I felt as though I was being pulled into the limitless darkness. Even the blazing white light bouncing off the walls around me couldn't break the gravitation. Time slowed as quiet engulfed me. A loud pop grounded me once again and I saw that the little girl's balloon had popped. Her arm dropped and something horrible began reverberating around the whole room. It sounded like something right out of the bowels of hell. Wailing and screaming pierced my eardrums like a needle through the skin. As the sounds of suffering grew, a chilling and rumbling voice came from the little girl, reprising her previous sentence.

"CALL HIS NAME!"

Hundreds of gashes appeared on the girl's body. Copious amounts of blood began gushing out of every pore. Her skin appeared to melt as something could be seen moving around inside her deteriorating form. Her face ripped in half and a long slender pair of hands pulled it apart to reveal the dark creature I had grown so tired of seeing. The body it emerged from turned to dust and disappeared. I had suspected it was just a guise to get close to me. I stared the creature in the face, unwavering.

"What are you?", I asked firmly.

The creature held its hand out and a strange book materialized within its palm. An electric surge shot through me. Whatever this thing wanted was in this book. I was at a stalemate with myself. Between those pages could be an answer as to why this thing was pursuing me...

Or it could be the key to my demise. I couldn't let my journey end this quickly.

"WITHOUT YGGDRASIL WE FALL"

The familiar guttural whisper echoed around me. I felt my temper rising. I was so sick of not having answers.

"What the hell do you want?! WHAT IS YGGDRASIL?"

I had my theories of course, but for some reason, I figured I could garner an official answer from the monster before me. Obviously, it was like shouting at a wall. My voice was still hoarse from trying to gain an audience with The Pillars.

I let out a long sigh. The creature had not moved since crawling out of its vessel, but the whispers casting themselves from its being grabbed my attention. I thought I had hallucinated it but I could have sworn I heard a name. I lifted my hand towards the creature and slowly approached it. I slowly rested it on the chest of the creature and the whispers stopped.

For the first time, the creature spoke from its rotting mouth. It uttered a single word but it sounded entirely different than the whispers I had always heard.

"Astaroth"

It promptly let out a loud bellow before disappearing into thin air, once again leaving me alone in the silent light.

My hand remained out in front of me as I tried to gather the pieces of the past 30 seconds. As it finally fell, I knew what had to happen next. I turned toward the screen and with what remained of my voice, I shouted out the name that was spoken to me.

"ASTAROTH!"

The 3 beings on the screen ceased all movement and turned their attention to me. The middle Pillar raised its hand and curled all of its fingers into its fist. What remained was an index finger, pointed directly at me. Some sort of energy struck me at my core and I was blasted out of the room I was in. I ended up in my basement. I quickly grabbed my chest to make sure I wasn't suffering from a heart attack. Everything had faded from my vision. The Pillars, the white room, and the stalking beast were all gone. I was back in my home. I stumbled over to the nearest wall and thrust my hands upon it. I had to make sure everything was real. As I regained my breath and balance, I was left with a feeling of uncertainty. I had no idea how I had gotten into that council or that room. I knew that sleep deprivation had something to do with it. I knew that my anchor allowed me to achieve the state I was in when it happened, but the steps necessary to achieve that level of vividity, and how to get exactly where I needed to go, were lost to me. I didn't know how I got from my table to my basement. I then remembered the parts sitting outside of my house. I knew they had to mean something. At the very least I knew I should get them inside in case any raiders sought to acquire them. I wobbled up the steps to the main floor. The light seeping in from outside was blinding. It was as though I hadn't seen it in years. Perched still on the table, was my Anchor. I had apparently left it while I was in my dream state. I flung the front door open and took in a huge breath. The air of the wasteland wasn't the greatest or the most abundant, but it felt needed. I slowly let the air leave my lungs, savoring every second. Breathing the air surrounding the planet was a rarity as it had grown so thin. I never wanted to imagine the day we would lose it forever.

I was hoping that the knowledge I gained from the Pillars would erase my cravings for atmospheric oxygen. I slowly opened my eyes and my mind was clear. I put aside recent events and began carrying parts in. Many of them were exceptionally heavy, and I was surprised that I could even lift them. I figured the machine that called itself Valiance, made it as such. I hadn't pondered it much and was still in the dark about where it could have come from. Was Valiance acting alone or was something bigger pulling the strings? The craftsmanship of that machine was clandestine and offered up no clues as to its creator. I kind of shook my head at the thought, still not in full belief of its existence.

All of the parts were laid before me. I let out an exhausted sigh as I gazed upon the mess of machine parts before me. I had a vision of my basement and a giant machine within it. These parts obviously had something to do with it. I needed more guidance. I had decided that I would have to attempt a call to Valiance once more. Until then, I would attempt to reconnect to the Pillars with my anchor. Hopefully, that name would work this time. I grabbed a piece of paper and hastily scribbled the name 'Astaroth' on it. I didn't know if I'd be able to remember it once I fell into that dream state again, but at least I'd remember it every time I'd wake up. I ran my hand along one of the pipes and another vision of the final construct crossed my mind. It had grown blatantly obvious what had to be done, however, I had no idea how all the parts were held together. Thousands of screws and pins adorned the ground. I'd be fumbling for years if I didn't know where they went. I wasn't an engineer or an architect so this task seemed monumental. I elected to once again leave them until I could consult with Valiance. I brushed my hands off on my pants and cast my gaze over to the kitchen table, where my Anchor sat. I saw movement. The most heart-sinking thing that can happen to a person in the wastes is the death of their Anchor. This fact became all too real as I witnessed a single leaf drop from the stalk and drift slowly to the bottom of the Esperata it was contained in. I ran over to it, in my haste, I bumped a mug situated on the kitchen counter, sending it careening to the floor. The shattering of the clay reminded me of the fragility of life within our choking existence as I placed my hand on the top of the Esperata. Breathing heavily, I stared, wide-eyed into the glass capsule, scanning for any more compromises to the structure of the plant. I rushed to the sink and obtained a glass of water. I returned to the Anchor and released the latches. I lifted off the capsule and began applying water manually to the roots. I quickly put the capsule back on top and latched it shut. I then checked the water levels inside the base of the Esperata and saw that it was empty. I was growing negligent in my obsession to fix this mess. If I continued to slip up in this manner, I could die before I got the chance to see what lied beyond the whims of my existence. Time stood still for a moment as it often did. Even the dust that was always visible in the rays of sunshine seemed to pause for my moment of thought. Was this my doing? Did time always stand still, awaiting my decisions? I took a deep breath and let out a sigh. I slumped down in one of the chairs and stared at my Anchor. I couldn't allow panic to overtake my thoughts. My brain was already in overdrive, whether it was saturated in profundity or insanity, was the blurred question. I cleared my mind and took in only thoughts of connection. I felt myself pulling away from my body as I did last time. The familiar glow of my anchor lit up the room as I once again disappeared into the void of uncertainty.

Chapter 6- A Reason To Dream

Zephyr Apherius- 24

    I cast open the door separating our HQ from the wastes. The sunlight was blistering. I was almost eager to get back in the truck and get moving. I always looked forward to the rushing wind. This was the first time we were heading to the facility in broad daylight. We wanted to see what kind of activity we were looking at in the middle of the day so we could analyze what we were up against. I finished tying up my boots and sat up. The thoughts of that dream were still fresh and one thing was burning clear. Something was on the horizon, and not something good. We were running out of time and I needed that time to re-establish the gardens. I knew that I could bring them back if I only had the means. Beyond the boundary line was hope. I was tethered to that hope and it drove me. I knew just as well as everyone else surfing this hell though, that hope was often a facade of despair. The probability was 50/50. I could find what I was looking for, or I could succumb to the harsh nature of the wastes. I would have no way of knowing unless I tried. I had to talk to Kash. I could no longer sit idly by while everything around me crumbled. If I could find someone I could trust out there, someone who knew the land, then maybe I'd have a chance. A shadow approached the open door and the silhouette of Kash stood within it.

    "Ready to go, Zeph?"
He seemed a lot more chipper than he had in previous days. I felt a small grin cross my face. It was so rare to hear the confidence in anyone anymore. It was always refreshing and always welcome.

"Yeah", I responded. For a split second, I felt that the world could be taken back from the invisible enemy. I looked up at him and felt the time was right to state my piece.

"Hey Kash?", I asked

"Yeah, what's up?"

I took a quick second to formulate my words as I wanted to make my case clear.

"I think it's about time I left the Maelstrom", I felt a jolt as I said the words. I was electrified. This was the moment I had forced myself to avoid.

"Zeph. I understand your desire to leave. I thought long and hard about what you said and I don't think that anyone should have to live the way we do, but there is nothing out there for us. There is emptiness beyond even our own."

I could hear the sincerity in his voice, he did seem genuine in his statement.

"How do you know, Kash? Because nothing has come over that canyon in the entirety of our lives? How do you know if there aren't people on the other side facing the exact same problems as us?"

Kash let out a sigh and dropped his head.

"I'm just trying to keep your best interest in mind".

This statement hurt me a bit. I had figured we all knew each other well enough by now. I felt a heat well up inside me.

"I'm not going to live my entire life in fear of the inevitable. If I die out there, I die. If I stay here, I die, it just takes longer. Taking risks is all we have left!"

"What do you think we are taking today, Zeph?! A risk to set us for life! We could live comfortably until our dying days!"

"And what about everyone else, Kash? Would you invite everyone else in? Or do you think we are the only sane people left in existence? If that's the case you are naive to think that this single facility can sustain our planet!"

Kash remained silent. He seemed disarmed, and the look he gave hurt me more than his last statement. The last thing I ever wanted to do was diminish the already dwindling confidence that this group possessed. However, to my surprise, I heard him chuckle, and then laugh.

"There she is!" He shouted. "You had me worried, Zeph! I thought we'd lost you for a second!"

I was confused by the turn of attitude but the mood was contagious and soon I, too, was laughing.

"So what's your plan?" he asked, still smiling.

"I thought you'd never ask", I responded.

I began outlining my plan to Kash. I would need a few extra oxygen tanks and an excavator on a motorbike. The plan was to use dugouts underground and much like a u-bend in a toilet, use water to trap oxygen in the pockets. I knew that the oxygen could dissipate into the surrounding dirt, so I opted to also apply a thin layer of plastic film to the walls of the underground. I would make a linear path of these dugouts towards the canyon. This would ensure that I wouldn't have to travel all the way back to the Maelstrom to replenish oxygen. I could spend my nights in these dugouts without having to worry about raiders. I would make my final dugout on the other side of the canyon where I would have 2 days of oxygen holed up. This of course would mean that I'd have no means to return to Maelstrom. I had accounted for that as well. One of my fellow Maelstrom comrades would follow me up in the truck and replenish oxygen. The truck could carry more than enough to sustain them for the journey. I had thought of using the truck myself but it would leave my friends stranded, plus there would be nowhere to conceal it once it reached the canyon, leaving us vulnerable to raiders. There were too many risks to bringing it for expeditions across the canyon. Kash seemed enthused with the idea.

"Well if we gain control of the oxygen farm, we will have full access to all the assets you might need! Well, what are we waiting for? Let's get us an oxygen farm!"

I could hear cheering off in the distance. It was Valian, exclaiming at Kash's remark. I was ready. I stood up and followed Kash out the door.

"We should probably tarp these", I heard Katya say as I approached the truck.

"How are we on gas?", I asked. I honestly hadn't checked in a while.

"Looking good it seems, unless our gauge is broken"

"Don't put that bad luck on us", I heard Valian say from the other side of the truck.

"What are you doing down there, captain superstition?", Katya questioned mockingly.

"Checking the tires. Don't wanna head out if there's a flat. You guys did zip out of there pretty quickly the other night".
We had been a little carefree in our escape as both Kash and I were certain we had witnessed something, not of this world. I had never really given much thought to the damage we might have caused to the vehicle during our exit. After his evaluation, Valian concluded that there wasn't much damage outside of some dings likely from kicked-up rocks.

"Look I know this is the apocalypse or whatever, but you should take better care of the thing", he said flatly before he began laughing.

"You're such a child", I claimed.
The time had come. We were riding towards new possibilities, and potentially a better life for my friends. As we loaded into the truck I decided to let Katya in on my plan. If anyone was going to be my follow-up to beyond the boundary line, it was her.

"You really are insane, you know that?" she said, giving me a friendly nudge.
She had always been the most understanding and often left people to their own devices if she was left to hers.

"We could find answers out there, Kat. This world could repair itself if we knew how to set it in motion".

38

This child-like hope kept me giddy and excited. Katya helped fuel it as well with her own thoughts on the future. We discussed at length what our world could be if the oxygen was restored. This conversation gave me a brief sanctuary as we approached the facility. Like all things good, unfortunately, the conversation was fleeting. We saw the facility peek over the horizon. Our destiny lied within. As we approached, all seemed quiet as it always had. It was easy to see the stories of weathering and wear on the monolithic walls. It looked as if they hadn't been tended to in years. In most instances this would seem as though the structure had been abandoned, however, in our predicament, this didn't mean anything. When survival is at stake, it would be easy, necessary even, to overlook maintenance. We pulled our guns out and stepped out of the truck. We made our way to the lot. We could seek cover in between the vans and see if any guards come out to make perimeter checks. The vans were unmarked so we had never had any idea what the name of this facility was. As the three kept their eyes forward at the main door, I looked up at the vans to ensure no one was hiding inside. Something else entirely grabbed my attention. As Valian and Kash continued forward, I held Katya back. She turned to look at me and I pointed up at the side of the van. I ran my finger along it and it came away with a thick layer of dust and grime. These vehicles had not been moved in quite some time, and the more I looked, I noticed that all of them were covered in the same grime.

    Could it be this simple? I stood up and began walking toward the front door. As I passed Kash and Valian, I could hear them trying to stop me. I halted and turned around.

    "Look at the vans, dumbasses," I said with a smirk. "There's nothing here."

I began jogging to the front door. I looked up to the security camera to find that it too had been collecting a layer of grime. I spun around once again and gave my friends an overly animated signal telling them that it was safe to approach.

As they approached, Kash rolled his eyes at me.

The only thing standing in our way now was a simple code lock. Valian elected to search the perimeter for a breaker box. Kash elected to go with him. If they could find a way to temporarily shut down the power, we could get in. Katya and I scoured the area for other means of entry.

Valian Sorik- 29

We moved around the side of the megastructure. I'd be lying if I said I wasn't stressed out. While Zephyr raised some good points about its abandonment, I still had my reservations. The grime vans proved nothing to me. Why would you need them if you were living in luxury with seemingly limitless oxygen? I'd have guaranteed that they had a singular vehicle hidden elsewhere. However, the surveillance camera was another story. I couldn't explain that. Zephyr had never led us astray before, and if Kash trusted her, I had no reason to doubt her. We came to what looked like an electrical box. I reached into my pocket and pulled out a cigarette.
    "Want one?" I offered.
Kash obliged and took one. I pulled out a match and lit them both up.
    "Man, what I wouldn't give to have a whole pack of these", he said.
Having access to vices was a luxury these days. I was nearing the end of my cigarette carton and was cursing the day that they ran out. Like the others, I often missed the simple times. I couldn't smoke back then, but I knew people could buy them as they pleased.
    "We took a lot for granted", I responded. "Savor it while you can"
He chuckled, pulling the cigarette from his lips and exhaling.
    "Let's get this box open", he urged.

I grabbed a pair of pliers and began pulling the metal panel away. I was greeted with a smattering of wires. I had no idea what connected to the keypad at the main door. I turned to Kash as he turned to me. This wasn't going to be easy. I could potentially electrocute myself as well. I had no idea how much electricity was flowing through here. I thought to cut them all and just reconnect them, but if anyone was inside, it could pose a threat to the girls who were scouring the area around the door. Cutting all of the wires could alert anyone inside and ruin our chances of surprise. not to mention I could trip any sort of security system. I began hearing a strange whirring noise and didn't think much of it, but as I turned to look at Kash I noticed he was listening attentively.

    "Do you hear that?", he inquired.

I had assumed it was something coming from within the building. Activated machinery or even ventilation ducts. The sand was cast into the air by the wind and as it blew around us, we heard the whirring grow louder, and as it did, it was paired with another odd sound that seemed akin to metal scraping metal. Kash made the call to find cover. Something was all too strange about this event. We sought refuge behind a large rock and we watched the building quietly.

    "We have to find Kat and Zeph", I told him.

    "They'll be fine, they know how to handle themselves. Keep your eyes peeled for movement"

I went around the other side of the rock and scanned for any oddities. Nothing. The sound slowly began dissipating until it faded into nothing. Kash shot me a look and beckoned me over. As he stood up, I knew that something was wrong. It all moved so quickly and in a blink, the leader I grew to respect and admire had fallen. Kash's body went limp and I saw that he had been stabbed clean through the head. The implement that came through his face was now pinned deep in the rock we took cover behind. I quickly moved my head to the source of the sharp implement and noticed it was attached to a giant mechanical monster. It appeared to have a similar shape to a scorpion. I was in complete shock for a split second. I was frozen in fear and disbelief. I had no idea what the hell this thing was. My body went into a sort of autopilot. I swung my gun around and began firing towards the creature. I got up and stumbled back grabbing the rock for leverage. I kept shooting and I finally felt the rage growing in me. My mind was finally taking in what happened. As I removed my hand from the rock to turn and run, I felt wetness. I looked down and saw that my hand was covered in Kash's blood. I began running, not turning back. My sole goal was to get to Zephyr and Katya and get them away from here. Or maybe it would be better to keep this thing away from them. I spun around to shoot at the creature. It was indeed pursuing me and it was gaining fast. There was nothing I could do. If it caught up to me I would be finished. The only thing keeping me from the grips of death was the adrenaline coursing through my body. As I rounded the corner I saw them. Katya and Zephyr! I didn't have to get their attention. I imagined that the screaming and gunfire would do that for me. Sure enough, they too began running towards me and began firing at the great metal beast behind me. This slowed it down just long enough for me to get behind another rock. I caught my breath and began opening fire once again. I heard Zephyr shout and it kicked me into overdrive.

"Kat, Val, keep it distracted I have an idea!"
I then saw her promptly bolt off. I had to get back up to Katya. She couldn't handle it alone. I stood up and felt a searing pain up my right leg. I looked down and noticed that a huge gash had opened up and I was rapidly losing blood. The shock must have left me numb to the pain. I knew that this wasn't the time to succumb to it. I gritted my teeth and began running to Katya.

"Nice of you to come back!", she said with a wild grin spread across her face.
Normally I'd have a snappy remark to throw back at her, but my mind was replaying Kash's death over and over again. I still couldn't believe it. I didn't want to, but there was no sense in falling to delusion. This was no time. I pointed my weapon and opened fire yet again. This thing was not going down. I saw Katya turn to

me, likely concerned that I had nothing to say in retaliation to her snarky comment.

"Valian!", she shouted.

I turned to look at her

"We're gonna be okay!"

A part of me knew that she was already aware of Kash's fate.

Katya Malikov- 25

It was clear that we wouldn't be taking this facility with a full party. I always liked to think that we in the Maelstrom have an unspoken connection. An unspoken ability to know when something is wrong within the balance of the group. I was hoping that it was just the giant scorpion thing messing with the vibes but I felt like something had pried our little family apart. I had never seen Valian like this before. He was pale and wide-eyed. Something like this couldn't have phased him this badly. I didn't have time to ponder as my thoughts were invaded by the sound of a blaring truck horn. We immediately snapped our heads to the source and saw that Zephyr had elected to use the truck as a weapon. She was always so reckless, yet she always seemed to come out of anything unscathed. She was on a direct collision course with the creature. I made it my goal to keep the beast still and focused as Zephyr rammed it from the side. I focused fire towards its eyes, an act that it didn't take too kindly. It let out a terrifying screech and made a motion to charge but it was too late. Zephyr landed a direct hit with the truck sending the creature flying into a giant stone. I watched her clamber out of the wreckage. She was bleeding from the head and stumbling around. It looked to me like she was concussed.

Zephyr raised her gun and began spraying bullets at the creature.

"Zeph, are you alright?", Valian shouted.

"I'll live, pay attention, this isn't over!", she bellowed back. The machine had re-established its footing. It looked rather damaged but one fact still stood. It wasn't dead. These guns were useless against it, so I took a different approach.

"Guys! I have an idea", I shouted.
I saw them both look towards me

"My turn", I said under my breath.
I ran out in front of the beast and grabbed its attention. I was hoping that the damage done to its limbs would give me enough of a speed advantage to get to higher ground. As I ran I grabbed a large stone and made a beeline for a bleacher-like structure. I climbed up and removed my oxygen tank. The machine was still pursuing me. I just had to let it get close enough to fire. I slammed my oxygen tank onto one of the metal bars in the bleachers and raised the stone over my head. I aimed the bottom of the tank at the machine, and made adjustments according to its movement. It moved closer and closer. I was getting antsy. I only had one chance. When it was finally in firing range, I brought the stone down on the oxygen intake valve, successfully creating a small missile. As it connected with the giant machine, a grand explosion lit up the area and pieces of the machine began scattering across the sand. A couple of fires blazed as everything settled and besides the crackling, all fell silent. My vision became blurry as oxygen starvation began plaguing my body. As I collapsed and faded, I saw Valian running towards me.

Zephyr Apherius- 24

Valian rushed to aid Katya with a new oxygen tank. The beast was destroyed but unfortunately so was the truck that got us here. My worries weren't too high as we had a whole parking lot full of new vehicles if we needed to head anywhere. My worries lied with the whereabouts of Kash. I had not seen him since before the scorpid machine attacked. I feared the worst. I knew that Valian had the answer and that I would receive it very soon. My head was pounding as I wiped some blood away. I sat down in the sand and began taking in some deep breaths. I saw that Valian had begun making his way over to me. As he approached, he asked,

"You okay, Zeph?"

I nodded weakly

"You were crazy back there! You saved our lives, thank you.", he added.

"Where's Kash?", I asked lucidly.

Valian's face dropped.

"I-I'm sorry, Zeph".

I had to see for myself. There was no way he could have fallen to such a thing. He was far too good to die. My mind was in a jumble with the events that had just transpired. This world was cruel. Far crueler when things are looking up for someone.

"Where is he"

"Zeph, you don't want to see the st-"

"WHERE IS HE?!", I screamed. "Show me now, Valian! Show me now!"

Valian stood up and held his hand out to me. I looked up at him and took it.

"You should get Katya.", I pressed.

"She's resting".

Valian agreed that Katya should also get to see Kash once she awoke. We began the walk back to where Valian said they were hiding from the creature. It felt like the longest walk of my lifetime. Marching towards a death that wasn't my own. It was uncertain. It was surreal. As we approached the rock I half-expected to see Kash jump from behind it and prove to me that this was all just a terrible dream.

That moment did not come.

As we rounded the corner, all my fears manifested into reality. Kash was pinned by his head to the rock by what appeared to be a giant mechanical stinger. He was lodged in. The only way he could be moved was by removing his head. This was a true defeat. Never had I seen such a beacon of inspiration or hope disposed of in such a gruesome undignifying manner. I was angry with the world I called home. I was filled with rage at the injustices that had befallen my people. It was people like Kash that gave me the fire to press on. In his honor, I swore I'd destroy anything that stood in my way of attaining our dreams. I would crush fate beneath my feet and take control of it however I saw fit. As all this welled up I saw images of my father's final moments flash before my eyes.

Not another one.

I began wailing, as tears of the most concentrated sorrow ran down my face, I felt the tight embraces of Katya and Valian. They had wrapped me in a tight hug as they too began to let their emotions falter.

"I promise you, Kash, that I will bring back the gardens. I will restore this world to what it was and I will bring justice to every piece of scum that stands in my way!"

Chapter 7- A Walk In My Mind

Llaric Ephyon- 35

    I found that I had torn away to a dark street. Rows of Victorian-style lamps lined the only path. The smell of rain was fresh in the air. I peered down at the cobblestone beneath my feet and watched as water ran through the spaces between the glistening rocks. I appeared to be entirely alone. I couldn't see past the wall of light emanating from the lamps. I felt as though another unseen power was preventing me from seeing beyond the street I was on. Furthermore, the only direction I could force my body to move was forward. I elected to go with it as I really had no other choice. The street took some light curves and as they crested, I noticed that some of the meticulously placed street lamps were missing, giving me a clear glimpse into the swallowing darkness.
    An overwhelming urge to shout into it came over me. Perhaps I had just longed for contact after walking the same path for so long. I had forgotten just how long it had been since I had seen another face. One like mine at the very least.
    The creature entwined with me was the only company I was ever in and it was far from welcome. I held my tongue, however, and pressed on. The rain began falling harder, as I approached a hill. At its crest, I could see the peak of what appeared to be a roof. I started the climb as the water began to soak through my clothing. As I walked I heard the sound of a second pair of footsteps. Had I been followed? That would be the only logical explanation as there was no other way to travel. Something in my mind told me not to turn around and to press on. As I did, rifts began opening on both sides. I ignored them. I didn't want to look into them. I only had

one goal in mind and that was to reach the Pillars that had previously eluded me.

Step, step, step

The side of a building became visible. It looked like an old hotel. I decided to seek shelter from the rain there.
Another set of rifts opened up, and out of the corner of my eye, something grabbed my attention. I stopped moving, and a final step echoed behind me. I wanted to turn around but I could not. I was willing to bet that the creature was behind me, shadowing every step. My attention however was more focused on what I saw in my peripherals. I forced my head to the left and looked into the rift. There, lied a man in a piercing white room, very similar to the one I was in while I watched the Pillars speak. He was laying in the fetal position adorned in white robes. He looked disheveled. His head was covered in long, slightly matted hair. His beard looked to be growing out of control. It was an odd contrast. As though his clothing had regular upkeep but he did not. I noticed he had his body wrapped around something. Upon closer inspection, I noticed that it was an Esperata. Was this man from my world?

"H-hello?", I called out without a thought, and to my surprise, the man weakly turned to look at me.

"Help me. It hurts so much. Iyatiroh is in great pain. Help me!"!
I pulled my gaze away, eyes wide, and heart racing. This man had just seen me. I have never been able to make contact with anyone through the rifts. His words crescendoed into a scream. I winced and covered my ears until it stopped.

"Llaric.", I heard him say. I hesitantly brought my eyes back to the rift to find his face encompassing the whole thing. It startled me a mite, but I looked at him.

"Get help for Iyatiroh. Find his friend Kairos. He will know what to do."
I remained silent for a moment. Was he able to hear me as well?

"I-Iyatiroh?" I asked.

His mouth curled into a smile showing two rows of decaying teeth. He nodded furiously and pointed at himself.

"You need Kairos?"

Once again he nodded, maintaining his strange smile.

"Kairos will h- help Llaric", he stammered.

"Who is Kairos?", I asked.

His smile faded and he cast his eyes down a little.

"The Dream- Keeper. He resides within."

Iyatiroh pointed towards the hotel with one long, boney finger. He began to laugh and dance around the white room that he was contained in.

It was obvious to me that this man had lost his sanity. Could it be possible that he too was plagued by an incessant demon? I slowly turned away as Iyatiroh continued dancing and clapping. I pressed on up the hill and a full building came into view. The grand doors at the front were a welcoming sight. I made my way over to the building and got up on the old wooden stairs, the awning above stopping the barrage of raindrops. I reached out towards the handle and twisted it. As it swung open, the scent of old wood came over me, and the dim lights within showed me the interior of the old building. My hunch was correct, I was indeed within a hotel but the layout was rather puzzling. I couldn't locate a front desk and there was no one around to make inquiries to. I began exploring and found that the rooms were located in a seemingly endless hallway that stretched into infinity. Stranger still, was that none of the rooms were numbered. As I moved through I couldn't help but think this was just a cruel continuation of the cobblestone streets. Everything in this building looked like it had been maintained rather well which contrasted how empty it seemed.

Scratch, scratch

What the hell was that? I naturally assumed that the scratching came from behind one of the countless doors. It ended as quickly as it came so I had no way to pinpoint its exact location.

Scratch, scratch

Louder this time. From behind me. I swung around and saw that one of the doors was shaking. The wood repeatedly rapped against the door frame. It was gentle but undeniably moving. As I approached, the door violently swung open. Much like the land beyond the lamps outside, it was nothing but sightless darkness. The sound of more doors opening echoed from all around, I made darting glances and noticed that every door in sight was now standing open. I was completely unprepared for what came next.

 Countless thousands of spectral beings sluggishly floated out from the abyss behind the doorways. They were… people. Emotionless expressions painted every single face that drifted by me. The beings were simply pouring in and staring into other doorways. It was still ominously quiet for such a packed hallway, and none of the people seemed to be paying any mind to me. I tried to grab one of them to ask where I was but my hand went right through.
 "You won't be able to communicate with them that way" The voice came as a shock as it was the only one I had heard since the Pillars. I turned to its origin to find a man standing before me. I was lost for words. A real, flesh-and-blood person was standing before me.
 "You'd think it was quite rude too if someone had their hand through your shoulder"
I looked over and realized my hand was still through one of the spectral beings. I quickly removed it and placed my other hand on it. It was cold.
 "S-sorry", I stammered.
 "How is it that you are here?", He asked.

"I was actually hoping that you could tell me.", I replied
He tilted his head at me. He was clearly discombobulated by presence.

"I have never seen another corporeal being in my realm. How is it that you can hold this form in the dream plane?"
Is that where I ended up? I had slightly understood the concept of astral projection but never thought that it could apply to my current state. I also seemed to lose a small portion of my memory when I split from my body. It always seemed to omit from my mind the fact that I could be dreaming.

"I- I don't think I'm sleeping", I told him.

"Projecting wouldn't change the form you take here. Unless-"

The man had trailed off and once again began pondering my tangibility.

"Are you Kairos?", I asked.
The man seemed to take a defensive stance against my question.

"How did you know that? Have you been sent to dethrone me?".

"What? No. You're the dream- keeper right?"

"You HAVE come to dethrone me! I won't give you the title!", he shouted.

"I don't want your title!", I shouted. "Iyatiroh told me your name", I responded.
He froze and looked at me.

"Iyatiroh?"
I nodded in confusion.

"How is that possible? He went missing centuries ago."

"He said that you would help free him".

"And how do you propose I find someone who has vanished without a trace?"

"I have no idea, but he seemed to be in tremendous pain", I stated.
I then remembered his odd toothy grin and his happy dancing.

"Well, he seemed to be in and out of a lot of different states", I added.

I explained my experience of the rifts to him and the nature by which I was able to speak to Iyatiroh. Kairos seemed to grow rather inquisitive about this man.

"Who is he?" I asked.

"He was the first dream-keeper"

"What is a dream-keeper?"

Kairos seemed eager to humor me as I appeared to be an exciting anomaly to him

"We dream-keepers preside over the dream plane and ensure that traveling souls aren't devoured or destroyed by the beasts within the threshold."

He continued by explaining to me what the dream plane truly entailed. The threshold acted as a protective barrier, protecting beings from the exposure of dangerous manifestations. In other words, these spectral beings could not cross through any of the doorways in the endless hall we were situated in. The dream-keeper essentially presided over this barrier and upheld prevention protocols, blocking realms from bleeding into one another. According to him, simply looking into the doors would show the specters a series of pictures that played out a story. This is the sequence of events that cause the phenomenon known by many as 'dreaming'.

"So what is it you are here for?", he finally asked.

"I am searching for three beings that came to me last time I projected. I have not been able to locate them again. They called themselves the Pillars of Light"

Kairos brought me over to an odd-looking pedestal and placed his hand over it. A series of words and pictures projected around us like a planetarium.

"This is the dream directory. Here I have access to prior dreams and memories of anyone or anything that has ever passed through here. The Pillars are in quite the predicament these days", He said.

"Wait, you know of the Pillars?"

"There aren't many that don't. They are widely believed to be the beacon of light itself. I have fragments of their memories and dreams but not a singular location. As entities that pre-date us, Keepers, documentation is scarce. What is it you need that would cause you to seek counsel with them?"

I looked over at Kairos and couldn't formulate an answer. One word escaped my lips.

Transcendence".

I saw a smile crawl across his face.

"Ah, that brings me back to the Trials of Knowledge"

"You've transcended?", I asked.

"I mean, I am the dream- keeper"

"Do you have any inkling as to where the Pillars might be?", I questioned.

"There are things beyond even me. The only thing that may help you is this"

Kairos procured an audio rendering that seemingly played only static. I then heard the sound of a growing scream. This scream evolved into a single static-laden word.

"ASTAROTH!"

It was my voice. My scream.

"This audio was picked up on the receiving end of your shout"

"Meaning?"

"Meaning that this was recorded in the chamber of the Pillars. Its origin goes far beyond the parameters of my directory."

He raised his hand and pointed to a small dot that appeared to project outside of the planetarium sphere that the directory created. I stepped outside the perimeter of the sphere and looked up. The pinpointed location did indeed pierce through the sphere into unknown space. The lonely little dot left me with more than a few questions. Could it be possible that even the dream plane, like space, had an unobserved expanse of unknown proportion? I also had to wonder if this plane of existence carried through time. Who knew if the Pillars were still with us or if their essence was just echoing from long ago. There was much to ponder, but one thing was clear… I was getting closer. Little by little, bit by bit, the answers were coming to me. Then something dawned on me. What if someone else desired the same thing as me? One with a pinpoint location?

"So does this thing work like a computer?", I asked

"Essentially, yes. It's a neural network connecting all breathing organisms to a centrality."

"So can you pull up people based on the nature of their dreams?"

"Of course", he replied.

"Can you pull up anyone with dreams of transcendence?" Kairos swiped his hand over the pedestal and began moving his fingers as if there were a keyboard in front of them.

"There are countless results", Kairos concluded.

"How about a proximity check?"

"To the current position of your corporeal body, there are four. A Vaskyr by the name of Soko, a fellow keeper named Ensifel, A lost man named Masis, and a girl?". Kairos seemed puzzled.

"Something strange about that?", I asked inquisitively.

"Of the four, she's the only one located on your planet, and not far from your current location."

This was such a stimulating occurrence. Everything Kairos said left me with more and more questions. What was a Vaskyr? He mentioned a fellow keeper as well.

"That keeper", I started. "He was your predecessor?"

"No no. This man, Ensifel is the keeper of something else entirely. I do not know much of him but I do know that he has spearheaded some sort of universal defense force. He'd probably be the best bet to get you to the Pillars. The Vaskyr girl, Soko is in his employ as well."

"What is a Vaskyr?", I inquired.

"Records show that they are an ancient race of proto-angels with the ability to level worlds"

An image flashed in my mind. The same one I saw while I was in the council with the Pillars.

"THE FIERCE ONE ROAMS"

Could that be her? The message on that stone said that this being could level worlds. If this were true, however, it would mean she is incredibly dangerous. Or perhaps the person that put the writing on that stone is just her enemy? Everything was getting too confusing, so I chose to focus on the task at hand. Locate these four beings, starting with the closest one.

"What was the name of the girl on my planet?"

"I can't get an exact reading on where she is, but it says her name is Zephyr Apherius."

Zephyr Apherius? I had never heard this name before. Even given the fact that she was in close proximity, and on my planet, it would still be like searching for a needle in a haystack. People were so few and far between, that I could end up going entirely in the wrong direction.

"Good things come to those who wait, Llaric Ephyon", Kairos said. It was the first cryptic thing to leave his lips since the fruition of our conversation. I immediately felt a pull as the familiar fading presented itself again. Everything was disappearing from view leaving me in the black void. I blinked and when my eyes reopened I was once again sitting at my kitchen table, the dying glow of my anchor casting the last of its light around the room. As it faded entirely, I realized that it had grown dark outside. I felt weak but somehow managed to pull myself out of the chair and make my way to the front door. The time had come to once again speak to Valiance.

Chapter 8- The Things We Hide

Zephyr Apherius- 24

It had only been mere hours since we lost Kash. The tears running down my face had since dried to my skin, painting a semi-permanent reminder of what we were fighting for. We had finally managed to get the main doors open and get a peek inside the facility. The room was dark and dusty. I knew at this point that it had been completely abandoned. The question of how long, was the mystery. Valian located a light switch and with a loud click the lights flickered on. We were standing in an office. A few of the desks were upheaved and various office supplies littered the dusty floor. Only a couple of the computers were still intact. Towards the back of the room, there was a large vault door.
"Great", I thought to myself. The last thing we needed was more hold-ups.
 "Katya, do you think we could blast this door with another tank?", I asked impatiently.
 "I wouldn't advise it. On the chance it does work, there could be more oxygen pods in there. We could lose the facility not to mention our lives if the chain reaction is big enough"
 We have a plasma cutter back at base", Valian pipped in.
 "Where and when did we get a plasma cutter?", Katya asked in disbelief.
 "Lots of raiders, lots of stuff"
Katya shrugged in agreement. And continued to look about the place.
 "In the meantime", Valian continued, "There might still be some active surveillance behind the door. Maybe we can access it via one of these computers."

He approached one and attempted a boot-up. The computer whirred as its fan kicked on. I came around to see what Valian was looking at. The screen switched on and through the layers of dust, the word 'Bios-Alpha' shone through. I looked down and noticed that it was password protected. The hint given underneath the entry point for the passcode read: 'Top Secret'.

I directed my focus to the filing cabinets and rushed over to them, pulling open any drawer that wasn't locked. I turned around and ran out to the wreckage of the truck. I wanted to see if there was anything I could use as a crowbar. I began pulling away loose metal to get a better look inside the vehicle. I found a hammer wedged between the seats and I reached in to grab it. I managed to wrap my fingers around the head of the implement and pull it out of the wreckage. I made my way back inside the facility and back to the filing cabinets. I jimmied the claw end in between the cracks of the drawers and pulled. A loud pop signified the lock breaking as I cast the hammer aside. This caught the attention of Valian who seemed at his wit's end trying to guess a password.

"Did you find something?", Valian asked.

"The hint said 'top secret'. I'm thinking one of these files might hold the key we're looking for. Have you found anything?" Valian brought his hand to his face and rubbed it.

"Well, the corporation that monopolized oxygen before everything went to hell was called 'Bios Alpha', and that thing that killed Kash. It was a guardian drone sanctioned by DRAIDA. We must have tripped its defense protocols".

DRAIDA was a name I had heard before. They were at the forefront of mechanical evolution and artificial intelligence in their prime. The stories state that they became so advanced, that they found a way to traverse realms and station themselves in other realities. I wasn't sure if I believed the stories, but in the world crumbling around me, all things were starting to look possible. I flicked through the folders to see if I could locate anything confidential. I removed 3 with the labels in question and tossed them onto one of the overturned desks. I cracked open the first one and I was presented with the image of a corpse. The documents following, depicted an experiment wherein corpses would be reanimated to utilize different respiratory methods. Within the pages, I saw that it was protocol to conduct the tests after death was induced. This company was forcefully killing patients to test their theories, and judging by the fact it was labeled 'top secret', that these patients weren't voluntarily advocating the procedure.

At the top of each page, I read the words 'Project Synthesis'. They were literally trying to reformat our respiratory systems. I was torn between feeling disgusted and proud of Bios-Alpha for attempting anything to preserve our species.
I turned my attention to the next one.

'Project Glass Shadow'

This document outlined some rather intriguing claims. Namely the manifestation of what they labeled 'dream beings' in our plane of reality. It seemed like Bios Alpha had been attempting to thin some sort of dimensional barrier between our universe and another. One of the documents continued to say that researchers were aiming to seek refuge elsewhere from the rapidly depleting oxygen. This project also included tests on the new visitors, these so-called 'dream beings', as well as tests conducted on their own personnel. According to those assigned to this project, communication with the beings proved rather difficult. I could tell from a couple of typos, that these tests were being documented hastily. They were beginning to panic. It was surreal to put all these emotions to a single date. The amount of fear and desperation that must be contained in the ink of these documents would be immeasurable. The testing pages I saw wouldn't add much comfort either, but I read on.

PROJECT GLASS SHADOW
INTEGRATION PROTOCOL

11.08.2534

SANCTIONED BY: BIOS ALPHA CHIEF EXECUTIVE ADMINISTRATOR

DAYNON SOROS

TESTING CONDUCTED BY: BIOS ALPHA THETA SECTOR LABORATORY

DR. LEN CORVUS, HEAD OF THETA SECTOR
&
DR. THEODORE APHERIUS, THETA SECTOR AGENT

SUBJECT 267
&
MK-00796

FIRST REPORT- 11.20.2534

"Subject 267 appears to be in a lucid yet reset state after the third contact with MK-00796. The being in question seemingly has the innate ability to transfer matter in its entirety from one fixed point to another. It would appear that Subject 267 is transported to the exact same location every time he comes in contact with MK-00796. Attempts to alter this location have failed. Moving forward we alter the meeting place of the two subjects to monitor any changes. No sign of successful integration"

SECOND REPORT- 11.25.2534

"Subject 267 has been eliminated by some unknown force, however has manifested back in his starting location. Encounters with MK-00796 continue normally. As expected, Subject 267 reacted violently upon discovery of his own body and worked himself into a panic. This panic appears to have roused MK-00796, but any attempt to place the 2 entities together for integration is halted by the unseen force that continues to eliminate Subject 267."

THIRD REPORT- 11.27.2534

"There has been a successful integration between Subject 267 and MK-00796, however something else has interjected itself into the equation. The resulting being has been noted as lethargic and unmoving. The body of Subject 267 has distorted and his flesh has succumbed to some type of necrosis. Attempts at communication have once again failed. The one silver lining is that whispers can be heard emanating from the entity. However, only one phrase appears to be discernible.
  "Without Yggdrasil we Fall"
Monitoring continues.

FOURTH REPORT- 12.06.2534

"I can't deal wih this anymore. I have begun seeeng the hybrid creature in my nightmares instilling the utmost fear in my heart. I have seen it in my quarters in the dead of night haunting me. Motions have been made to terminate the prokject.

FIFTH REPORT- 12.10.2534

"The hybrid has been disposed of but it still plagues me. My colleqagues have brought similar stories to my attention. The whispers... The fucking whispers. They won't stop!"

[TEST END]

My heart skipped a beat as I read the tail end of this report. I knew exactly what this 'Hybrid Creature' was but had no idea it was a product of testing. I dropped the file in terror, kicking up dust from the derelict floor. My chest heaved with every labored breath as the file folded closed revealing the words 'PROJECT TERMINATED', on the back cover. Katya rushed over to analyze the commotion.
    "What's wrong?"
I slowly looked over at her with the same contorted expression I made when I dropped the folder. Not breaking my gaze, with her, I called out to Valian with a choked-off, wheezy sounding voice.
    "Try Glass Shadow"
I heard the clicking of keys behind me and much to my mortified chagrin, we were in the Bios Alpha System.
I could feel an uncontrollable shuddering race over my body. Katya gave me a comforting rub on the back as she too cast her eyes down upon the now dust-covered folder. She managed to coax me over to the computer to see what kind of monsters these people were. Valian scrolled through hundreds of cataloged tests that I assumed were all just as messed up as the one I had just read. We looked through the contents of the computer until we found the surveillance feed. We quickly pulled up the one labeled vault and we were shocked at what we saw. A metal holding tank of biblical proportions was the only thing that lay inside. This whole time I thought it was some sort of military hub housing thousands of soldiers, but I had been wrong. It was an entire oxygen farm. Ninety- seven percent of this building was a damn oxygen tank! Were they hoarding this or using it for their "research".

"Well we've got our answer right there", Valian said pointing to the screen. "All we need to do is head back to HQ and move house. That plasma cutter will get through this bad boy. Then we can see if they were hiding any Anchors in there" he said walking over to the thick vault door and giving it a bang.

"Firstly", he continued. "We need to get the power back up and running and change the code on that door. I would like to re-route the wire that powers it but we don't really have access to the tools needed. I'll jumpstart one of these Bios Alpha vans and head back to base and grab what I need. You two hold out here and see if you can dig up any more information. Maybe a location that could lead us to some more people".

Katya gave him a nod as the thoughts of that folder still ruminated in my head. Valian headed out the door and it closed with a crisp bang.

"What did you see in here?" Katya questioned ambiguously.

"The Umbra"

"Wait. You mean that thing you saw in your dreams as a kid?"

I could see that she was beginning to connect the dots about what was contained in that folder.

"They were fabricating nightmares?"

"Not exactly", I responded. "They made an attempt to jump ship and find sanctuary in a new reality. Or integrate other things with our chemical makeup to see if we could thrive in this environment."

Katya looked at the other two folders still situated on the overturned desk.

"And those ones?"

"Just as bad", I choked back.

Katya flipped through a few of the documents.

"These guys are all kinds of fucked up", she told me as she continued reading. "They were just gonna leave all of us to die in their last-ditch effort to save themselves"

"What?" I asked. I had not read the third one.

"Yeah. Project Necroterra. A lot of the info has been redacted and it looks like some of the pages are missing but the gist of it is the eradication of life on the planet essentially."

"It would seem they have quite a few secrets hidden", I responded.

I made my way over to the computer to see if I could get any more information about the calamity. Numerous files were labeled with codes of some sort, or perhaps subject numbers? I clicked on the 'emails' tab. The window opened and showed that the email belonged to a 'Lumis Goodwill'. The body of the last sent e-mail only had one sentence:

"The Eclypse will not falter!"

"Kat, come check this out"

Katya made her way over to the computer and looked over at me."

"The guy wrote one sentence and misspelled eclipse."

"He was probably in a hurry to get out of there. This was written around the time the apex of the panic was ensuing.

"Did you read the message string?" she asked.

"This was the only message in the thread", I responded

"Can you find who it was sent to?"

I scanned the screen for a recipient of the email and noticed that it had around 500. This email was broadcast to hundreds of people. I couldn't tell exactly who they all were but numerous addresses succeeded with @biosalphacorp.com. Were these colleagues? Superiors? What was the motive behind this email? It was greeted with static silence too. It was strange indeed. I closed the window and moved the cursor to a folder that read 'Confidential'. I clicked it to see if the name on the email came up. I was prompted to enter another password that would direct me to the Bios-Alpha mainframe. This would likely connect me to other facilities and could potentially put me in danger. I decided to avoid this avenue as accessing the mainframe could likely give outsiders access to us. I knew there was some way to mask our activity but that wasn't my specialty.

63

"Hey Kat, see if you can find anything under the name Eclypse"

"You have a hunch?", she asked.

"Not yet"

Katya gave me a little smile.

"Always so mysterious".

Chapter 9- Will You Answer The Call?

Llaric Ephyon- 35

I stood barefoot outside as the rain came down. Another rarity. I pondered ways to conjure up the great machine I had seen a few nights ago. I had remembered that Valiance seemed to have a gravitational attraction to the lights outside my home, so I made my way over to where I first saw him. I traipsed through the sand, feeling it flow between my toes. It was always a comforting feeling, especially now that I was trying to summon a giant machine for blueprints to another machine so that I could have answers about the first machine. It was all very convoluted, and I suppose that also helped to quell the anxiety that was trying to pound my heart right out of my chest.

    I reluctantly reached up and flicked the first light on. As I proceeded to the second it was as if my mind grabbed me by the shoulders asking me, "What the hell do you think you are doing?!", but I ignored it and pressed on. I flicked on the second with a wince. Did I really want this? What if its intentions are different this time?

    No.

I couldn't afford to let human fallibility get the best of me. The survival of my species was at stake. That thing that I saw constructed in my basement through my visions held a pinnacle key to all of this. I needed to know how to construct it. Once I did, I might be able to locate this Zephyr girl and figure out what all of it means. I flicked on the third with a little more confidence in my motions. Nothing could stand in my way anymore. I could not allow it. Before I knew it, every light had flicked on and I was greeted with the same familiar booming noise and green flash that I had seen in my previous encounter. I stood my ground and watched as the silent giant floated around the corner at the far end of my property. The orange glow of his eyes cast my shadow behind me. I began walking towards him. Then his voice came to me as it did in my pod.

"What answers might you be seeking?"
I responded with confidence that alarmed even me.

"I know what I must build, but I don't know how to build it." Valiance looked at me and then at the stars. I could tell, even through those mechanical eyes that something was bothering him.

"Home", he started. "Is relative. I foresee you building many with others yet unknown to you."

"I- I don't understand"

"Will you answer the call, Llaric Ephyon?" Valiance asked me, bringing his gaze back down to earth, squaring his eyes directly on me. Was he speaking of the signal I encountered with Kairos?

"If I say yes will you give me the knowledge to build this machine?"

"You already have it. Yggdrasil awaits your full integration." Those final words stuck in my mind. A blinding beam of light erupted from the sky and enveloped Valiance. Was that really how he made an exit? He might as well have painted a giant target on my back. Then again, I was the one who took the risk and turned on every light outside in the dead of night. With one final woosh, The light had dissipated taking Valiance with it. I had grown accustomed at this point to gaining several questions each time I encountered another living being. I bet by the end of this, I would be comprised of nothing but. However, the one thing at the forefront of my thoughts was that I already possessed the blueprints for this machine. I raced inside after killing all the lights in my yard, and situated myself, once again, in front of my anchor.

I focused my thoughts on the visions I was having about the machine. This time I wasn't pulled from my physical body. Instead, I started receiving new images. They were blueprints! As it began piecing itself together in my brain, I found that I had memorized most of them. I broke my tie to my anchor, grabbed it, and rushed to the basement. I set it down on a dingy, decrepit, wooden shelf. I positioned it in a way that would allow me to work without my breathing apparatus getting in the way.

I grabbed a piece of sheet metal and began forming it to the necessary proportions. I had let my brain take over, putting my body into autopilot. I could not believe that the very thing I had been seeing in flash images in my mind was now coming to tangible fruition. I was putting piece by piece together as if I had done it a thousand times over. With this minor disassociation, I was able to mull over other thoughts I had earlier. What was the call that Valiance had seemed so eager that I answer? He made it sound as though I would be among many people who I would someday call friends. I understood the 'Home is relative' aspect of his statements. Thoughts of a true nomad perhaps? Come to think of it, did Valiance have a home? Where was it he disappeared to when he was taken away by the sky-born light beam?

It was as though these questions were my long-time friends walking a perilous journey with me. I looked over at the clock, then let out a re-grounding chuckle. Time was no longer a crucial concept in my mind. At this point looking at the clock was just habitual. I no longer had the need for sleep, so counting the hours of consciousness was moot. Every time I returned from a projection I felt just as well-rested as if I had slept for twelve hours. What was time really, anyway? A construct established to segment our lives. There's a time when we work, there's a time when we sleep, there's a time where we have the day off to stimulate the economy. We were all slaves to something that we had created, and when we run out of time, we are left blaming ourselves for the things we could not do within its confines.

I was on the cusp of something grander than the desire for fame and fortune that many possessed in the old world. Something that many would say they didn't have time to research or time to comprehend. I felt a smile grow on my face as beads of sweat dripped from my forehead onto the floor. Whatever this thing did, had to be connected to me and Yggdrasil. My integration with this entity is somehow crucial to the role I play later on. At least that's what I gathered from my conversation with Valiance. I always got an answer one way or another. All I have to do is wait. Build and wait.

  I set down everything and made my way upstairs. The sun was cresting over the horizon once again. The nights no longer felt endless and I was constantly invigorated by theories. I had revisited the idea that Yggdrasil was a connection between all living things and my hypothesis now included living things between all realms. The reason we see things in our dreams is because of Yggdrasil. Kairos had outlined the process very clearly. I admit the idea that everything that we see in our dreams is real, and has the potential to cause us harm, still shook me a bit, but with Kairos at the helm of the threshold, I was confident in knowing that sleeping souls would remain safe. I also had the thought that Yggdrasil might be intrinsically tied to the dream plane, or might even be synonymous. If that were the case though, I'm sure Kairos would have had more answers for me.

  Perhaps Yggdrasil was a cut above the dream plane, incorporating even the beings that Kairos fought so hard to keep out. After all, the directory couldn't locate a signal that I was certain came from a living being. Yggdrasil must have been the messenger for that transmission.

At any rate, I would continue the construction of this machine and see what functions it holds upon its completion. In the meantime, I would attempt to conjure the rifts again. Hopefully, I would be able to communicate with whoever was on the other side. I looked over at my anchor which I had brought back upstairs with me and wondered if it needed watering. I walked over and pulled out the side compartment. Still full. I looked up at the plant within and gave a small nod of assurance as I picked it up and brought it back downstairs.

"The answer does not sleep", I thought to myself. "Good thing I don't either".

Chapter 10- Blind Goddess

???- ???

"Does he seem capable to you?", I heard her say from behind me.

"He shows promise", I replied flatly. I had not seen Llaric Ephyon in person for what seemed like decades, but I had been silently monitoring him for quite some time. The glow of the hologram cut through to every dark corner of the room, giving off a dubious flicker. I stepped away from the pedestal and turned to her. Though her eyes were always covered with that cloth, I could always feel them watching me, almost smiling.

"Do you reckon he'll make it here?"

"The answer is already foretold, Seraphim", I said with a slight bow.
I returned to my normal standing position and saw that she was now smiling at me.

"Fate is never concrete, my apprentice. On the contrary, it's more like a sail that bends with the winds of fortitude."
I was always one step behind her. Like a goddess of foresight, she always left me in the dust when it came to understanding.

"And I told you, you can call me by my given name"
She had always attempted to get me to use her original name.

"That would be a great sleight to your accomplishments, Seraphim. After all, how could one so kind, and so insightful fall to the feelings of hopelessness"

"Always so formal, my child", her voice sounded warm as it always did.
I owed her everything. She had saved my life and in my mind, the least I could do was forfeit it to her. She was an icon of the highest

caliber, and I devoted everything to ensure her existence was as comfortable as possible.

"What about the other one?", Seraphim asked me

"Zephyr Apherius. Her heart is strong and her resolve is stronger."

"Their meeting would signify evolutionary success."

"I hope you are correct. Will Valiance be back soon?" Seraphim smiled once again. It was always infectious.

"He shall return soon"

Chapter 11- Setting Out

Zephyr Apherius- 24

"I'm going to head out tomorrow.", I told Katya. I was finally embarking on my mission to reinstate the gardens. I swore that I would have Anchors sprouting once again. We were fortunate enough to have access to numerous vehicles now, so my trip would be easier. The vans looked like they could carry about as much as the truck did. Once I got to the canyon, I would have to use a bike. From there I could take three or four oxygen tanks across with me. Hopefully, the other side would harbor some fertile soil.

    I would await Valian's return so that I could say goodbye. This was it. I was going to get this done if it killed me. I had already set up the plan with Katya. I was taking more than enough oxygen with me. It would only take 1 day to get to the canyon. She was coming with me on the bike and taking the van back. We elected to bury some tanks in the event of an emergency, and after 2 days she would intercept me in case the bike couldn't make it back up the canyon. I still had questions about the nature of Bios Alpha and the role they had played in the collapse of the world. We heard the growing roar of an engine as Valian returned. The van gave a few strained growls as it trudged through the sand. The door opened and Valian let out a small groan as he pulled himself out. We went out to greet him, and with a tired nod, he closed the door of the van.

    "Grabbed a couple of things for dinner" he said, producing a few canned items. We all gave it a mildly disgusted look but knew that there weren't really any alternatives. He handed the cans off to us and went to the back of the van. I saw him take out the plasma cutter he was clamoring after as well as one of the bikes from our base. I had requested he bring it for my voyage. I was honestly surprised that he managed to get it into the van.

"How's the ol' base?" I heard Katya ask him.

"Still intact. Didn't see any raiders crawling about trying to take anything. We'll see how long that lasts."

I hadn't seen raiders in quite a long time personally. I was wondering if their numbers were beginning to dwindle like the oxygen around us. Dying out like the fading atmosphere.

"I also brought some more weapons", he added. "Never know when we are gonna need some firepower", he said motioning over to the scarped machine that now lay in pieces. I asked Valian if he knew a way to hide our IP address on the computers so we could check files on the mainframe. He gave me a nod and promptly headed inside. As he worked I told him that I would be leaving the following day. He looked up and gave me a kind of hurt smile.

"Well when you asked for the bike, I figured it would be one of these days. Stay safe out there, 'kay?"

I smiled.

"I will"

Valian turned back to the screen and began flicking away at the keys. I made my way outside and grabbed a gas can out of the back of the van. Gasoline was another rarity in the wastes. I was surprised Valian was able to procure any considering the scarcity of vehicles around these parts. I was actually convinced that we held most of the automobiles in the quadrant. I made my way over to the gas tank at the rear left side of the vehicle. I pulled open the tank door and unscrewed the cap. As I inserted the nozzle I looked out into the lonely desert and breathed in the sandy air. This would be my home for the next few days. I wanted to get acquainted with the smells and the sounds before I left…

It might be the last time I experience them.

After the tank was filled to the brim I made my way inside, where Katya had already pried one of the cans open and was devouring it like some sort of wasteland animal. She looked up at me with some level of shame. Her eyes begged me not to judge her for her actions. I knelt and gathered some provisions for my journey. As I made my way to the door for what felt like the fifth time, Valian's voice echoed through the room.

"I'm into the mainframe. We are completely incognito"

I shot my gaze over in his direction.

"Search anything under Eclypse"

Valian let out a labored sigh and responded.

"I have a folder labeled whistleblowers"

"Is that it?", I responded quizzically.

"That's it. I'll give it a look"

I heard the conformational click and then the scrolling of the mouse wheel as Valian took in the unknown information.

"It looks like there was some sort of family issue with this Eclypse thing".

For some reason, this piqued my interest.

"Was it a, 'Something Goodwill?'", I asked without a thought.

Valian remained silent for a split second before responding.

"You've already found something on them?"

I recounted the email I read earlier.

"One Lumis Goodwill sent out the final email from this facility", I said with a high level of conviction.

"He had a brother"

The words came over me like an ocean wave. The guy who apparently held a high stake in this company had a brother.

"What?"

"Lumis Goodwill had a brother and get this, his brother was the one who founded the rebellion group, known as Eclypse"

"His brother? You mean?"

"They were once against each other. Lumis' brother Solsta spearheaded the uprising against the old government", Valian said coldly.

Then, everything about Eclypse came back to me.

74

I remembered the day the government fell. My father was beaming with joy. It was as if he was awaiting a new overtaking. I remembered him offhandedly discussing the Eclypse when I was a child, but I never thought much of it until now. Was my father a sympathizer? I honestly had no idea what Eclypse even stood for. Either way, I had no intentions of believing my father was a malevolent man. The Eclypse seemed to propagate a benevolent message:

    "Rise above the injustice"

But that was about it. The news always seemed to snuff it out, before it could blossom into any sort of collective. As I grew I found myself becoming less aware of this group as it faded into obscurity. Perhaps my father wanted me to stray away from the influence of this faction. Yet I couldn't help but wonder if they were still kicking around. A group that had the strength to dismantle and extinguish the entire government had to be around still. Right?

    "You should get some rest, Zeph. You've got a long drive ahead of you tomorrow. You too, Katya".

Katya gave Valian a pouty expression. Something a child would give their mother in protest. She stared at him hoping to change his mind. After no response, she reluctantly unrolled her sleeping bag and crawled in. She turned over to look at me. It almost felt like the sleepovers I had when I was a kid. She smiled and pulled her hand out of the sleeping bag and formed it into a fist.

    "We got this, Zeph"

I smiled and bumped her fist with mine. I faded into unconsciousness moments later to the sound of computer keys clicking.

    I awoke in my old living room with an Esperata between my arms. The respirator was a little tight. I sat up and rubbed my eyes and proceeded to adjust the straps. The television was still on and the sun had long since disappeared to slumber behind the mountains. I must have passed out watching TV. I scoped out the dark room and heard footsteps from upstairs. The hall light flicked on as the footsteps then began making their way down the stairs. A man came into view. I had no idea who he was.

"My sweet daughter", he said. "What are you doing up so late?"
I had no fear. Something told me that this man was my father. I knew at this point that I was dreaming because although this man looked nothing like my father, I felt safe as if I had known him my whole life.

"I just woke up, Papa", I said in a squeaky, high-pitched voice. Was I a child again?
Was this another memory playing back to me? If so I didn't remember it, and it would mark the first time my dreams didn't feature my father as he was in life. I got up off the couch and picked up my Esperata and began slowly pacing the living room. I looked up to the mantle above the fireplace and saw a framed certificate.

'In Recognition of outstanding achievement'. I knew that something had gone awry in this memory. For one I don't ever remember my father possessing any certificates of achievement. As I looked down at the name, the bold print seemed to mock me, as if to rub in my face that I'd never see my father again...
The name on the certificate didn't read 'Theodore Apherius'. It read a name I had never heard or seen before in my life.

'Llaric Ephyon'.
I turned once again to look at the man that appeared to portray my father.

"It's time for bed, Ophelia", he said gently.
I looked up with wide-eyed wonder at the man as I began to proceed up the stairs where a black void greeted me and transported me back to consciousness.

I rolled over in my sleeping bag and looked up at Katya who had somehow jerry-rigged some sort of primitive coffee maker. She must have heard the rustling because she turned around to where I was sleeping and whispered

"Want some coffee?"

I wearily nodded as I sat up.

"There wasn't much, so don't tell Valian we drank it all"

I laughed and Katya abruptly brought a finger to her lips, she then pointed over to a now sleeping Valian. The bickering computer screen bouncing off his unconscious form.

Katya brought over a crudely bashed-together tin mug filled to the brim with piping hot coffee. The smell was enough to kickstart my brain. Much like anything in this world, coffee was a luxury to have and was meant to be savored. I cautiously grabbed the mug from her so as not to spill any, and took a tiny sip. Bliss. Even black coffee which I used to despise was a respite from the daily hell that we were forced to live. Katya had a small lantern next to a giant sheet of parchment. One of her many maps no doubt.

"Whatcha doing over here?", I whispered.

"Trying to figure something out before we leave"

I looked down and realized that she was constructing a blueprint of the facility. We had been unsuccessful in locating one within the filing cabinets.

"Something doesn't add up", She stated. "There are a series of pipes that seemingly have no function. I have pinpointed every wire and every pipe to its function, but there is a small bundle of them that just seem to disappear into the ground with no purpose."

"Perhaps they were abandoned during construction. Improper placement or something"

"Maybe," She replied, uncertain. "Either way, it'll have to wait 'til we get back. Let's wake up this lazy sack of bricks", she finished already over Valian.

She dropped down to her knees and turned to me with a dubious grin. She once again put her finger to her lips as she turned back to Valain. She then let out a huge bellowing "AREN'T YOU EVEN GONNA SAY GOODBYE TO US?!"

I swore I saw Valian jump two feet in the air from a lying position. I immediately began howling as a rush of joy took me over. Valian's eyes were wide and he was breathing rapidly. His head snapped directly over to Katya who had moved back to avoid a punch.

"Dammit Katya, you're such a bitch" he growled.
Both of us were on the floor and Valian began to pull himself from his sleeping bag.

"Don't tell me you made all the coffee too"
Katya brought her mug up to her face and gave it a little shake. Valian looked defeated.

"Don't worry big guy, I saved you half", she said, shoving the mug in his face.
He let out a long sigh and took it from her. It looked as though he forgave everything after that first sip as a look of sheer ecstasy took over his face. As we all sluggishly got ourselves together, I made my way outside to the van to load some tanks into the back. I ensured that both vehicles were filled with gas and made my way back in. Valian was already back at the computer typing away looking more into the causes of The Shift. We had hope that we could potentially run into Eclypse during our travels. A chance to link up with more people was always welcome. I was sure they would need something else to do. If I could run into them by chance, I might be able to convince them to help me establish the gardens. As we said our goodbyes to Valian, I hugged him and so did Katya with a sarcastic sort of sigh.

"See ya later dumb-dumb. I'll be back in a couple of days."
Valian threw his arms in the air.

"Freedom!" He shouted. You could tell he was going to make every moment of his time alone count.
I opened the door and a jolt of adrenaline ran through me. The first course of action was to locate fertile soil. After that, I would have to locate Anchors or anchor seeds. I would not fail. I could not fail. I hopped into the driver's seat of the van and looked out to Katya who was checking the bike. She looked over at me after she clambered on and gave me a confident thumbs-up. I put the van into gear and felt the crunch of the sand beneath the tires as the vehicle proceeded forward.

Chapter 12- First Contact

Llaric Ephyon- 35

My fingers were raw and cut up. I was nearing the completion of the machine. Exposed wires were organized neatly with zip ties. Blue lights flickered through grates in the giant structure. I looked into one of the reflective panels and noticed that my face was covered in black grease. The ground was littered with the remaining pieces. I still had no idea as to what purpose it served, but now would be no time to stop. There was an odd transmitter of some kind within the main cabinet of the machine. It was fixated towards the sky above, but something told me this wasn't sending or receiving transmissions from space. I wiped away the sweat from my brow with the back of my hand and let out a quick huff. I looked up the stairs. Light was pouring through the crack of the closed door. The stairs felt like a monumental task to overcome, but I made my way up anyway. I stopped to look once more upon the beast I was creating. I couldn't help but wonder if this was all truly worth it. I made my way to the washroom and pulled out some loose bandages. I looked into the mirror as I began covering up my wounds. My face was beginning to look more gaunt. When was the last time I ate? There was that word again. Time. It would seem we couldn't shuttle through life without its mention. An inescapable gravity that has the power to wear away your face, your muscles, and your sanity. Time leaves you in withered atrophy. I looked down at my now bandaged fingers and made my way out of the bathroom and into the kitchen. I opened the fridge. Most of the food within was already overtaken by mold and rot. I closed it and turned my attention to the freezer. Inside was a block of ice and what looked like an old, freezer-burnt slab of meat. I had no idea how long it had been there. It was then that I realized I could be in trouble. I had completely neglected my basic needs in pursuit of these answers. I set the bag down and placed both my hands on the counter. I had not been grounded in weeks. I was risking my life by leaving the lights on all the time too. While I hadn't seen raiders in quite a while, I was still pulling some extremely risky moves. I began to breathe rapidly. I had gone into a panic. New thoughts were flowing into my head, which I thought was going to explode. It was as if two souls were vying for control of my body, completely refusing to coexist. I ran over to the sink and keeled over it. The sensation to vomit was overwhelming. As I gagged, though. Nothing came from my mouth. Man, I really had been avoiding proper care. As I finished, I turned still breathing at a quickened pace, I slid down the side of the counter to the ground. I had gone too far. I felt like death was knocking at my door. Was something knocking at my door? As the two versions of me fought over my body, I could have sworn I heard a rapping on my door. Checking it could either be suicide or insanity. I'd either be greeted with a series of bullets, or the crippling emptiness of nighttime. The knocking grew louder. Voices started replaying in my head. I could hear Kairos, Iyatiroh, and the Pillars murmuring endlessly until a high-pitched, blood-curdling scream overtook them. It was clear to me that this was my daughter.

"Ophelia!", I yelled through the splitting pain in my head. All at once, everything ceased. As I opened my eyes, I was greeted with a horrific sight. That monster that I hadn't seen since our last encounter in the white room knelt next to me. Its sunken, glossed-over eyes piercing my very soul, instantly killing the battle within me. I slowly moved my head down my body where I felt a cold pressure on my left leg. As my head stopped I could see a large, decaying hand placed gently on my thigh. I looked back up at the creature who was silent for the first time in my life. Had it just staved off the voices and screaming? I let out a deep breath.

"Th-thank you", I stuttered.

It lowered its head slightly and to my surprise, it nodded. It pulled itself up in a terrifying sort of squatting stance and stared at me. Much like in the white room, I approached it and hesitantly placed my hand on its shoulder. I was shown the flash image of a woman fighting her way through the wastes. I then saw her standing before a fallen friend, wailing in agony over her loss, blood matting her messy black hair. Two others came into view and held her while she cried.

"We're so sorry, Zephyr", I heard one of them say.

Then I was back.

As my kitchen became once again visible I could see that my arm was suspended, but it was no longer touching anything. The creature had gone. I lowered my arm and felt a tear run down my cheek. Was I...?
That girl was Zephyr Apherius. The one I was seeking. The one who would help me save us all. I couldn't tell where she was located as she was constantly surrounded by sand. She could be anywhere on either side of the canyon. Perhaps I could reach her through the rifts or even her dreams. If that was the case I might be able to give Kairos enough information to triangulate a position. I had spent far too long cooped up, and hiding away. It was time to go searching for the keys to a higher existence.
I reasoned with myself first. I knew I had to eat. I looked back at the frozen slab of meat on the counter. It would be a few hours before I could cook it. I turned to the front door where I had just earlier thought I heard knocking. I picked up my Anchor and headed outside into the crisp nighttime chill. I sat down on the steps and stared out into the desert. For the first time since all this had occurred, I was relaxing. I had a powerful craving for a glass of scotch at this moment. One of the rarest treasures in these times was alcohol. What I wouldn't give for just a sip. I closed my eyes and imagined the taste. A weak smile overcame me.

"Oh well", I thought to myself. "Once this is all over we probably won't have any need for it anyway".

A distant orange glow commanded my attention. At first, I thought it was Valiance bringing me more words of incoherent wisdom. I chuckled a little bit. Everything was always so cryptic with him. The glow turned into four separate lights. They were torches. People were moving through the wastes! I immediately figured they were raiders. Off to the east were the ruins of a large city. Malvora was once a bustling metropolis supplying this end of the country with all its goods. I would often see a convoy of government vehicles traveling through the desert to the Bios-Alpha facility across the canyon. I often believed the only reason I was spared death was because I chose to live in seclusion with Ophelia. It was an all-out war in the city when the Eclipse came about. I never entirely disagreed with how they dismantled our government. Especially now. In my opinion, the Eclipse just quickened the inevitable. I rarely ventured in the direction of Malvora, as hordes of raiders now called those ruins their home. As the orange glow continued moving East, I wondered if they were raiders or innocents who had no idea that they were marching towards their demise. I couldn't risk finding out. With the state I was in, I would be dead in seconds if it happened to be raiders. My leg began shaking, and I buried my head into my hands. I was wasting away. The pains in my stomach were ever-growing as reality layered itself over me like hundreds of blankets. I felt the panic returning. I could not allow this. The perceptions I was succumbing to could not be allowed to override my current objective. I smacked the sides of my head to bring myself back to the surreality I was previously living. It honestly felt like banging an old television to get rid of the static, but as stupid as that sounds it actually helped a little bit. I stood up and brought myself back inside where I stood still for a couple of minutes. My brain was attempting to recalibrate itself. I set my Anchor on the counter and placed my hand on it. It once again began glowing. The pain of starvation was evaporating out of my pores. I knew I had to eat at some point or my whole operation would be moot, however, the food I had resting on the counter couldn't be worked with until it was thawed and I had no practical way to speed up the process. I figured I'd try once again to get in contact with Kairos. I would have attempted to reach another one of the beings seeking transcendence through a rift, but they were much harder to conjure up in the conscious realm. A blinding light overtook me, and I was once again in the rain on that cobblestone path. The haunting lamps almost seemed to glow brighter than the last time, even further obscuring the darkness beyond. Once again my body was taken over by an unknown force, pushing ever forward to the familiar hotel. The doors to the great building swung open and I headed inside. I began my trek down the infinite hallway and located Kairos. There were already numerous souls floating through the doors lining the walls. He looked at me with a sort of half-smile.

"Llaric, back so soon?", he quipped with a hint of confusion in his voice.

"Hey, I saw her earlier. The Apherius girl"

"Did you discuss anything about the Pillars?"

"Well... I didn't exactly have the means to interact with her. She was shown to me by... it."

Kairos looked beyond puzzled at my statement.

"Come on, man. You know what I'm talking about don't you? The- the thing. The big creature that stalks me wherever I go."

His stare remained blank.

"Dammit Kairos, what kind of transcendent being are you?" A smile lit up his face and I could see the gears turning once again.

"The corrupt anomaly that has been rotting dreams. I have a tidbit of information that might be useful to you", Kairos told me with a little more vigor than normal.

"That Apherius girl you have been looking for has also been seen with this... it. It would appear she lovingly refers to it as 'The Umbra'", he said with a sarcastic chuckle.

"Umbra?"

The word umbra is commonly associated with shadows. More specifically the darkest points of a shadow. The word umbra is also used to describe the total phase of a solar eclipse. A shadow of biblical proportions encroaches on the planet until it is almost entirely engulfed in darkness. When the moon is directly blocking out the sun, the umbra is at its largest. It was a rather fitting name for the beast.

"Have you spoken to the others?", Kairos blurted, cutting through my aloof inner monologue.

"I haven't been able to open any rifts. I had an uh... incident."

"You can't fight those things, Llaric", he said, clearly eyeing the shape I was in. "If you waste away you can't maintain the bridge between your world and the next. These things, if ignored, can lead you to some very dark places. I've seen it happen to some prospective dream keepers".

"So what should I do? Going back and forth works me into a panic. It's like I'm going into shock with every transition."

Kairos rested his hand on my shoulder and pressed on.

"Much like the gap between our worlds, there is one between you and yourself. You must bridge it."

Why did I feel like he was about to pontificate on the value of self-worth and inner strength? Everything had become so cryptic and I wondered if it was because I was learning something, or if everyone I knew had all got together and just planned a large joke at my expense. I'm sure I could crack the codes. Between Kairos and Valiance, I had enough puzzles to last a lifetime, and they all needed to be deciphered. I elected to leave and attempt a rift conjuring. I knew I couldn't spend much longer here without satiating my primal self.

"Kairos, I've gotta go. I have one more thing to do before I fix the mess I'm in"

"I'm sure I'll be seeing you soon, Mr. Ephyon"

I nodded and produced what felt like an awkward grin. I quickly turned back and remembered that I had another question.

"What's beyond the lamps out there?"

Kairos looked at me speechless for a moment as if to gather his thoughts.

"In the darkness, one tends to need a light source to see. In some instances, conventional light simply won't do."

What was I thinking? I ask one question and he just hands me back a plethora of other questions. I let out a small sigh and turned around once again towards the front door. I stepped out and walked to the place where I had opened the rift to Iyatiroh. I closed my eyes and focused on the other three people that I had been shown in my previous interaction with Kairos. The Vaskyr girl stood out. Her hair was an unnatural hue, and she possessed a rare characteristic. Soko had heterochromia, a condition wherein the eyes of an individual are two different colors. I was told this was a common trait in Vaskyr and it was a trait shared by the Vyridia that used to live in Malvora before the fall of the Overseers. As a matter of fact, it was stated in an Eclypse rally that the two races were related. The public at the time was shown horrendous clips of the Vaskyr conducting numerous slaughters. They were told by the Overseers that these beings were actually the Vyridia, and this false information almost led to the extirpation of the latter race in Malvora. I was hesitant about establishing communications with Soko due to the intel I had on her species. I had no idea what kind of person she was, so I had to keep my distance until I could learn more about her. Unfortunately, this also ruled out contact with the Keeper known as Ensifel. Kairos had told me earlier that this girl was in his employ, meaning he could be even worse than her. I figured I'd attempt a connection with the man, Masis first. He had a kind face and a trustworthy demeanor. If we could aid each other, perhaps he might help me with the others. I opened my eyes and as expected, a rift opened before me. This was getting easier. At least in this realm, it was. Energy seemed to flow more freely here. Staring into the rift I saw the stone walls of what appeared to be a study. A coat of arms and various swords lined the walls. It was like staring into the dungeon of a castle. That was my belief until I panned my sight over to the glow of many large computer screens. Talking into these things was always strange. It always felt like I was speaking into a painting or a television. I always harbored some level of embarrassment during these interactions. There was no one in this room, however. So I decided to make my presence known.

"Uh, hello?!" I shouted into the rift. There was no response. No static. Nothing.

"Mr. Masis?"

The sound of a heavy wooden door cut through the silence and I was greeted with a couple of grunting noises as the person trying to push it worked their way inside.

"WHAT IN THE HELL IS THIS THING?", I heard a man shout. I could only imagine he was exclaiming at the giant hole in spacetime that I had just ripped in his study.

"Excuse me?", I started as an older gentleman shuffled into my view. A well-kempt hair-do and beard sat on his head as he tried to make heads or tails of the invasive anomaly before him.

"Who are you?" He asked, many degrees calmer.

"Hello, my name is Llaric Ephyon. I was led to you by the Dream Keeper, Kairos. I've been told that you are Masis, correct?"

"Well that is me, however, I have questions that outweigh mere introduction", he said with an inquisitive squint.

"I understand, sir. I-"

"How did you manage this?!", he interjected. "It's simply marvelous! Like a reality fabric phone call! Simply marvelous" His attitude was all over the place. I couldn't put my finger on any one emotion, so I decided to get right to the point.

"Transcendence is the reason I'm here before you today. I have been informed by the Dream Keeper that you seek the same thing as I do."

His eyes trailed off to the corner of his study.

"I've grown desperate, Mr. Ephyon. I've lived a lifetime of regrets and hardships and I have been clinging to the concept of transcendence like a child to its Mother. I'm afraid that's all it is though. A concept. Believe me, I have tried everything to achieve a higher level of understanding. I have spent many years in hiding from the Cersyan Order so I have had nothing but time to try."

I had no idea how to take the information. His statement didn't seem entirely plausible to me. I was both sitting in my kitchen ethereally connected to my Anchor, and out in the warm rain on an overly lit cobblestone street talking to this man, so I knew there was something he might be missing. I explained my situation to him and some sort of lightbulb went off in his brain. He abruptly turned to face me once again and uttered a single word.

"Archetype!"

Another word I hadn't heard. I was beginning to think he might be just like Kairos and Valiance. In on this big joke that would be the final nail in my sanity's coffin, but he accommodated me, and began explaining his story. I breathed a sigh of relief.

"Finally", I said to myself. "Someone who's gonna get to the point".

"What is it that drives you to study transcendence?", I asked him.

He let out a long breath. I could tell that this was a difficult topic for him, but he opened up anyway.

"Twenty years ago, I was employed by the Cersyan Order to keep the roster updated at their facility in Cersyus. I was to keep track of who came in and who left. I began to notice that there was a lot more coming in than leaving, so I decided to investigate. The things I saw... I wouldn't wish upon anybody. The despicable acts perpetrated by the Order on these... these children, they haunt me every night. I had no idea what was going on behind closed doors and now... so many. So, so many have lost their lives. I've been trying to find ways to bring them down. To find the light that would erase them forever... And then, one of their projects succeeded. A young man had managed to escape their ghastly clutches and wouldn't you know it, wind up on my doorstep. He's out now gathering intel on the Order for me."

I had felt a twinge of guilt for asking. The remorse in the old man's face had weathered into every line and wrinkle on his skin. This is someone who had been suffocating under a guilt of his own for so, very long.

"So you've been seeking transcendence for self-forgiveness?" I asked.

"Not exactly. What I want is to delve deep into the mind and find where exactly it rots when people do something as heinous as this. I am but one man and I've spent years holed up in this place like a coward. Transcendence would give me the ability to understand the minds of those in the Order, and potentially touch the strands of time and turn them back."

As Masis continued, he told me of the origins of this mysterious Order. Apparently, they had just arrived in his homeland one day and ever since, had been pulling their government's strings. They were highly intelligent and according to him were almost alien in that aspect. They brought highly advanced technology to a land that was not yet ready to appreciate it. The story reminded me of Malvora before the fall of the Overseers. DRAIDA, the multi-billion dollar tech company, had brought countless marvels of technology to that city and completely revolutionized it. The difference in my case was that the tech they were bringing in was meant for good. The Order that Masis was telling me about sounded like monsters. Another question crossed my mind.

"Do you know anything about the Pillars of Light?"
He squinted once again before shaking his head.

"That's a shame. I'm looking for them. I believe they'd be our best hope of achieving our goal."

"I will help you Mr. Ephyon. If we seek the same thing, then we can help each other."

I couldn't say much else. I was frozen. I blinked a couple of times before cocking my head to the side slightly.

"Then we shall be in touch", I told him. "Goodbye, for now, Mr. Masis"

His face was solemn. He pursed his lips as I closed the rift. He was the first person I had spoken to on the subject that wasn't either an omnipotent dream god or a terrifying monolithic machine.

Hope.

The word danced plainly off the walls in my head. It was almost strange to feel some semblance of positivity in these trying times, but I savored it for all it was worth. I pulled myself back to my body and found that the sun was cresting the horizon out of my window. I glanced over at the meat that I had previously placed on my counter and it was completely thawed. I turned on my stove and for the first time was able to return to my primitive self without falling into hysteria.

Chapter 13- The Parting

Zephyr Apherius- 24

The whip of the wind was exhilarating. With every breath, I feigned off a smile as my purpose drew closer and closer. Katya and I approached the edge of the boundary line. A strong electricity charged through me as I stepped out of the van. A thick layer of dust now lined the sides of the vehicle rendering the fading 'Bios- Alpha' text unreadable. I walked over to the edge of the canyon as the wind gently blew my hair into my face. This would be where I'd start digging. The sand seemed to stop about ten meters before the edge of the cliff, and soft loam and dirt took its place. During my inspection, I saw Katya join me at my side.

"So this is it, huh?"

"This is it", I replied.

"It almost looks like the edge of the world. As if whatever created it just stopped here."

She sounded rather stoic and I couldn't help but believe it was partially due to my temporary departure from the Maelstrom. Without warning, she spun to me and pulled me into a tight hug. It would appear my hunch was correct.

"Is there nothing I can say to stop you?", she said with a little sob.

"This is what I've always dreamed of doing, Kat. If I go beyond the boundary line, I will either find what I'm looking for or I will not. Either way, I can't just continue living the way I have been without knowing if there's something more. Besides, I'll be back eventually."

Katya's face twisted a little.

"We have just found new hope with Bios-Alpha, Zephyr. It could be the answer to all of our problems."
I felt a small heat ignite in my stomach.

"It will never be anything more to me than the place that took Kash's life. I refuse to spend the rest of my waking days hiding behind heavy metal doors in a fluorescent-lit office building."

She let out a sigh and a look of acceptance grew across her face.

"You were always the adventurous one. Who am I to take that away from you? Take care of yourself out there, okay? I'll be back in a few days to re-supply you."
I smiled as I once again turned to the endless pit standing between me and my dream.

The creak of metal rang out as we opened the back of the van and began unloading the numerous O2 tanks within. What a monotonous action. I feel I had spent the better part of my life loading and unloading tanks into vehicles. Did Katya really want to continue this way of life? She was always so lively and her choice to confine herself within concrete walls was very unlike her. Then again, everyone reaches their limit at some point. I'm sure the loss of Kash was weighing heavily on her as well as Valian. It's only natural to harbor worry for loved ones in a time like this. I admired her for the facade she was putting on. She continued to unload tanks even though I could tell it was killing her inside. She remained rather silent during the entirety of this.

When the van was cleared, we began digging holes in the sand to bury a fair few of them before I made my descent into the cavernous depths. I also made sure to leave a few tanks in the van for Katya. She returned to the front of the vehicle and spun around. We stared at each other in silence for a minute as the wind picked up slightly around us. The sound of sand hitting the van being the only thing we could hear.

"You'll be okay... right?", she asked hesitantly.

"Of course!", I shouted back confidently. "This world won't take me that easily".

She seemed consoled by my words. She looked down, seemingly trying to fight off her disapproval.

"I love you, Zeph", she uttered to me shakily.

"I love you too, Katya"

She nodded and smiled through welling tears, as she turned around and got in the van. She gave me one final look before turning around and speeding off over the sun-soaked sand.

I looked up to the sky. I reckoned I had three or four hours of daylight left. I figured it would be easy to spot anyone coming during nightfall as people needed light sources to travel these parts of the wastes. I let out a sharp huff before grabbing tanks and moving to my first location, six meters back from the cliff face. This would be my toughest hole to dig as I had to start from scratch. There appeared to be a cave system on either side of the canyon, so digging would be minimized. I set to work right away and began moving the soil from the ground around me.

After about two hours I had a dugout that could fit two people standing up. I was losing daylight and I was already exhausted. I knew I had to press on, so began digging into one of the walls of the hole I created. I tossed the dirt up through the vertical hole I had made. This would be the most dangerous step in my plan. The dirt could cave in on me if I made a wrong move, and I was also vulnerable to raiders if they came across the hole I dug. I had to be quick. I increased my pace, against the protest of my screaming muscles. Though my lungs were on fire, I continued until I had a short tunnel leading to a small alcove. Here I could rest from the night. I could tell the sun had nearly set. Everything was practically pitch black, luckily I had used the dirt from my small alcove to fill the opening leading to the hole I had dug earlier. I hoped that anyone who came across it would just assume it was a hole that had been dug out and then abandoned. The cave systems on the side of the canyon gave me a sense of solace. They seemingly had small collections of water within that I could eventually use for water traps. This would offer me an extra layer of security in my future dugouts. The water traps would help keep oxygen in my alcoves as well as render any firearms useless, should anyone come across them. I opened one of the four oxygen tanks and an indicative hiss let me know that it was flowing. I placed the breathing apparatus over my face and slowly let slumber take me over. The black swirling mass of nothingness welcomed me. My brain must have been in total shut down as on this night, no horrible creatures nor scathing memory befell my dreams. All was calm for once in my life. I took this peace as a sign that I had finally begun on my right path. My sleeping bag lay on the cold cavern ground. The rich smell of sterile earth wafting into my nose coaxing me further into unconsciousness. It was a surprisingly fresh smell and a familiar one at that.

When my eyes next opened, I was slightly disoriented. In the old Maelstrom base, we were usually awakened by the young rays of the rising sun. Underground, there was no telling how long one could have been asleep for. Even if they were to emerge to sunlight, there was an off-putting feeling that they might have been down there for longer than a single night. Regardless, I slowly dug my way out of my underground cocoon, stopping occasionally to listen for any sound or movement above. Eventually, I could see little beams of yellow-orange light cutting through the particles of dirt. It was some time after dawn, and with one giant scoop, the warm glow of the sun poured in from above. I pulled myself from the hole and stretched while looking around the flat, sandy landscape. There was almost something picturesque about these dull surroundings. I made my way over to the mound that contained my other oxygen tanks and tore out a few. I would devote this day to filling random caves in the system below before digging. Once I reached the bottom of the canyon, I could make an assessment on how to port more of them across. I had rope but needed something to anchor it to in order to repel down the cliff-face. I decided to comb the edge of the cliff for a while. A large boulder seemed like my only hope for the descent, however, the anchor I came across was much more unconventional to the landscape. I would first rappel down a series of oxygen tanks that I could use to make the rest of my journey. Afterward, I could pull them up the other side and make my way to solace.

Katya Malikov- 25

    I was driving on autopilot for the better part of the day back to base. I knew the wastes like the back of my hand. Ever since I was young I had a certain affinity for cartography and that sharpened my directional proficiency. Every chart we ever drew up, every map, we ever amended, every blueprint we scoured was overseen by yours truly. I was always so confident in my navigational prowess that I never thought there'd be an obstacle I couldn't tackle. Losing two of my own was the first instance that I was not able to since the shift began. As I drove, every bump the van took in the sand recalled the haunting image of Kash's body pinned to that rock. All for the sake of what? Some oxygen and some gruesome, yet useless pieces of information. I knew that Zephyr had this whole thing right. I was fully in agreement with her sentiments and the idea of a better life, or at least one with answers. I slammed my hand on the steering wheel.

Screaming.

    When I had first met her, we were quite a bit younger. I was already traveling with Valian and Kash. She had crossed paths with us in the wastes. She had grown malnourished and looked rather frail, yet we kept our wits about us in the event that it was a raider setup. She stared directly into my soul with the most lifeless expression one could muster. I sensed no ill-will from her. Her attention was pulled away from me by Kash who offered her some water. She snatched the canteen out of his hand and began cranking it down like a wild animal. She didn't even stop to breathe between gulps, resulting in a heavy panting. Her eyes scanned the three of us as she wiped her face. It was an altogether silent exchange. That was until Kash spoke up.

"Where are you headed, young lady?", he inquired.
She stared at him, blinking a couple of times but remaining silent. Kash decided to pry further.

"Where are you coming from?"
She slowly turned, never once breaking eye contact with Kash. She raised a boney index finger and pointed off in a vague direction. It was apparent she was suffering some sort of delirium.

"Are you alone?", Kash asked with a small wince, realizing that the question was a somewhat suspicious one. To our surprise, however, she spoke.

"I am"
Kash's face had curled up into a worried expression. He rounded the vehicle we were operating out of at the time and came back with one of our food provisions.

"Are we sure this is a good idea, Kash?" I questioned abruptly.
I was so stupid. Had I really been that selfish at one time? I'll never forget the look he gave me after uttering that ridiculous question. He looked more pained than Zephyr did.

"We aren't raiders, Katya", he began. "Our business lies in compassion for the ones who have nothing. You cannot build a family out of enemies".
Those words have always stuck with me, and by proxy so did Zephyr. As she learned to trust us, she learned to become part of the crew. While most of the time this was peaceful and whole, there were times wherein tough decisions had to be made. You'd never think it possible for there to be a time where you must take another life, let alone at the age of sixteen. However, she persevered and saved my life by making that impossible decision.

I owed her my life, and if it weren't for Kash's compassionate nature and her fate was left in my hands on the day that we met... I fear I would have left her to die. That's why I swore I'd do whatever I could to protect her, and here I was leaving her at the edge of the boundary line by herself. I was sick to my stomach at the thought of it. I wrestled outcomes in my head until the blaring lights of Bios-Alpha seared a hole in my retinas, successfully assassinating the warring thoughts that weighed on me.

As I kicked the door to the van open, Valian popped out of the building to greet me.

"Pretty neat, right?" He asked, spinning his finger and pointing to the personal sun mounted to the building.

"Why don't we just hook up like twelve megaphones together and shout WE'RE HERE, COME KILL US, into the wastes?" I retorted sarcastically.

"You coulda just said nothing", he said kind of off-put. He held the door open for me as I re-entered the building, rolling my eyes slightly. He went over to a newly wired fuse box and killed the power to the lights outside.

"Got any booze?" I asked, rubbing my eyes.

"Best I can do is pickle brine"

I felt disgust creep up my face.

"I did save you the rest of this though"

He pointed to the cup of coffee from the morning earlier.

"Got no way to heat it up, unfortunately, but I figured you wouldn't pass it up."

He was absolutely right. I jumped on it like it was the last coffee in the world and it very well could have been. As I drowned myself in the remaining liquid gold, Valian spoke again.

"So I did some more digging into Bios- Alpha while you were away, and found some interesting things."

"Oh?"

"Turns out this place did a lot of inhumane things in their final days. Most of their testing was conducted on a race of beings known as the Vyridia. Most of it was voluntary, but a lot of it was done behind closed doors it would seem. I also came across this little tidbit about our friends in that resistance group." He stopped a second before continuing.

"Eclypse was composed of members of the Vyridia race as well as sympathizers. There was serious turmoil in Malvora over the existence of these beings. The three Overseers that perpetuated this hate, fed the masses false imagery leading to the deaths of thousands of Vyridia. Eclypse brought down these Overseers and plunged everything into chaos. Things only got worse when they publicized the Shift. All surrounding districts fell like dominoes at the mention and left a lot of good people displaced or dead."

He almost seemed like an internet search engine for insanity. Yet a lot of the things he was saying really started to add up as to why we were in this situation. He beckoned me over to the computer and pulled up a video. It was simply titled 06.07.2532.

"Is that a date?" I asked.

"Twenty years ago"

He started the clip and two people could be seen giving a speech. Partway through, a disturbance could be heard. It sounded like a door being kicked open. Immediately following that was a man shouting. He was trying to stop something. He was trying to inform the masses that they were being lied to but was silenced as gunshots rang out in the background.

"The video is date stamped, but there were no obituaries anywhere. However, because I'm a big, smart boy, I found something interesting."

He proceeded to pull up a list of names and photos on the computer. Many were greyed out with the label deceased to the right of said photos.

"These are employees of Bios-Alpha and as you can see, their vital signs are monitored. Not only that but a change in their status is marked with a date stamp. Every deceased worker you see here has the exact date and time they died saved into the Bios- Alpha databanks."

"Let me guess, you found someone in there that matches the date stamp?", I asked in a jesting manner.

"Oh, not just anyone. The Chief Executive of Bios-Alpha, Daynon Soros", he replied with vigor.

"W-wait", I stammered.

"What's up?"

I had remembered the folders that Zephyr had showed me earlier and recalled something odd.

"Those top secret folders... those horrible projects were signed off by Daynon Soros"

"What's your point?"

"They were sanctioned in the year 2534. Two years after his death"

There was something strange going on all those years ago. It left me wondering what other secrets Bios-Alpha was hiding.

"Well ain't that a mystery", Valian finished with a crooked grin.

Chapter 14- Hell's Gate

Llaric Ephyon- 35

  My new objective had become clear. I needed to resupply. For the time being, I had to focus on my survival, yet the feeling was almost unrecognizable. The shift from a higher consciousness to a primal headspace was rather taxing. My surroundings felt alien. Like I had never seen them before. The nexus of threads and meshes that I once saw and felt, were now gone. The inside of my pod looked altogether different than it had in past months. The vibrance in color seemed to diminish slightly, almost as if a filter was applied to my vision. I slowly placed my fingers down on the counter and moved them along its length. My sense of touch was otherworldly. Not better... but different. The one constant between my states of mind was my Anchor. The energy I felt radiating off of it never changed, though its glow was now masked from sight. It appeared to be in good health, and I was glad that through all of this, its needs hadn't been neglected. I paced the rooms as I contemplated a strategy for gathering supplies. My mind was scattered. There were countless thousands of thoughts that until recently, had lied dormant in my brain. All at once, they raced around in my head, kicking off the dust they had collected while I was gone. I had to focus. Where could I find food? Where was I? Who was I? My daughter! I had a daughter? I had never really anticipated that I would forget certain things, or that I possessed two entirely different minds. How could I have put her out of my mind? My dear Ophelia. How could I have just let you disappear?!

Focus.

Malvora. The city is located east of here. Occupied by gangs of raiders. There I would find food. There I could resupply.

Slowly my thoughts collected themselves and neatly compartmentalized themselves. Memories started returning to me. I approached my front door and slowly opened it. I stepped out into the heat and turned the corner. A bike stood, almost buried in the sand. I had almost forgotten about it. I had been in another world for so very long. Several worlds for that matter. I was surprised to see it hadn't been commandeered by any passers-by. I had no idea if it was still functional. A light layer of rust began taking over some of its components but altogether looked well intact. I approached and began digging it out of its desert tomb until it was once again fully exposed.

I ran my hand down my cheeks. I looked over at where all the machine parts had once laid in my yard and saw shafts of wood from the pallets they came on. I approached them and located a rather large piece that came to a point at one end.

"It'll have to do", I told myself. It was very likely that I'd be attacked if I was spotted and I was alone. I'd have to analyze my options once I arrived. I ran inside and located a roll of tape, I used this on the other end of the wooden plank so as not to give myself any splinters while carrying it. I snatched up an old pair of goggles and set them down on the table near the door. I knew it would be wisest to leave at dusk under the cover of night. I truly hoped that the wind would pick up as well and mask some of the engine noise. I would have to dismount a couple of minutes out of the city so that no one would hear me coming. I had no idea if they had people stationed outside the city so I would have to take that into account as well. I suspected that my best bet would be to go around the outskirts and approach from the water on the easternmost end. Then again, there was no telling if the raiders had set up outposts. In that event, a direct approach to the west end would be safer. I speculated that there would be enough cover to hide me in darkness. The direct approach also offered me a quicker get away if things got out of hand. Yeah, that was my best bet at survival. I was rather ill-prepared, but I was determined. The wait for nightfall weighed on me. I couldn't help but take in the idea that I could soon be on the precipice of my demise. I tried to shake off the feeling, but its influence grew on me like an unyielding cancer. I hadn't even set out yet and I was already on the brink of hyperventilation. I needed to keep my mind busy. I rushed over to the door of my basement and swung it open. I barreled down the stairs and gazed once again at the machine I had constructed. It sat there, cold and grey, offering nothing. As if it closed off some sort of neural pathway and became nothing more than a giant, meaningless hunk of metal. Why had I wasted all my time on this folly? Had the fallacies been written at the behest of beings like Valiance and Kairos? Or were they too, just benign imagery to stoke my failing mind? I was the one suffering the delusions. They weren't put there by anyone else. Had there even really been anyone else?

Stop.

    I was running myself in two different circles. Feeding multiple minds with one primitive body. I needed to conserve my energy and focus on what would keep me alive in the moment. I needed to stop drifting around the planes of consciousness. I gave myself a couple of hard slaps on the cheeks and I was back. I feared that my mind was deteriorating and vowed to keep myself to one task. I told myself that until that task was completed, not to warrant any unnecessary thoughts. To keep my mind busy, I attempted to retrace my thoughts. I paced outside casting occasional looks at my motorbike. Watching as the shadows grew on the ground. Inch by inch. I had retained most of my memory. I remembered all of my time with my daughter Ophelia and the loss of her mother. I couldn't remember who her mother was or what I did for work. It appeared to me that my mind wasn't backward compatible with its transcendent state. It was like data was being corrupted, rendering it inexecutable in my memory. Tried as I did, I couldn't remember those two things.

The sun had finally tucked itself beneath the horizon. I pulled a jacket over my shoulders and mounted the bike. As I turned the key over, I smelled gasoline. The engine revved on and crescendoed into a confident growl. I coaxed it forward and pressed on into the night. I could pick up a scent in the thinning air. It had a pleasant, sweet aroma. I was encased in darkness as the faint lights of my home faded into the background. In an hour or so I would be at the edge of Malvora. I never thought I would see that place again. I had no idea what to expect. It had been twelve years since I had last been there. Who knew what kinds of things lie in store. A technological marvel, taken over by simple-minded raiders. I was laser-focused to the spot directly in front of my headlights. I had to monitor the area for obstacles or potential ambushes. I could see the orange glow of the city off in the distance. It looked like they had managed to keep the power grid online. Either that or they jerry-rigged some generators up to some portable lighting system. I had no recollection of the color of the street lights.

It had been so long. I was thrust back to the time I spent in the city. I saw her. My... wife? Her entire being stood before me in a rundown, mildew-ridden house. Her face was erased from memory. A blur was all I was given in its stead. Her voice rang out to me, but to my dismay, I couldn't make out what it was saying. I briefly saw a flash of black behind her before my attention was pulled away to a beaming little girl next to me. She was holding up what looked like an art project of some sort. On the bottom, it read: To Daddy. The lettering was something you would expect of someone her age. Messy, with some backwards characters, but otherwise endearing. Had she intended this gift for me? Ophelia. I loved that gift. I attempted to call out to her mother to show her what a great job our daughter did but every time I called out her name, it was suppressed. It was the only word escaping my lips that I couldn't comprehend. How could I utter a word and not know what was being spoken? My mind appeared to disconnect from my speech every time I tried. Eventually, the faceless visage of my child's mother spun around to take a look, and once again her words were stricken from my mental records. I could hear the praise through the redacted sentences, however, which led me to believe she was a caring woman. I blinked a couple of times as the kicked-up sand sprayed my goggles. I was surprised that in my current state of mind, there were answers I was still seeking. Answers that I had swept under the rug, hoping they'd turn to dust while I abandoned them to a higher consciousness. It was a vile feeling. Like I had fed their memory to the fires of hell itself.

Buildings.

    I could make out their shapes. All that I remembered had still been standing from what I could tell. The time had come for the second half of my journey into the city. I had located a myriad of boulders and decided to tuck my bike within. The rest of the trip would be taken on foot. I grabbed my makeshift shiv and pressed forward. If a raider with a gun apprehended me, I would take his weapon by force. As I grew closer, I could hear cheering and gunfire.
    "Really? This early?", I whispered to myself. It would be my luck that this short into the operation I come into contact with them. I was rather frail after having neglected myself for so long. I wouldn't stand a chance fighting one of them. My strike had to be lethal if I wanted a firearm. I slowed my pace and my breathing as I approached the west entrance to the city. Blown-out windows littered the streets with glass. I'd have to be mindful of this, as it meant that the glass had been blown out from the inside. There could be hordes of raiders in the dark buildings, poised for an attack. I ducked down behind a car and noticed a couple of voices

in the distance. I peeked around and noticed the dancing glow of a fire underneath a tarped-up fence. Shadows moved around in the warm shimmer. Raiders. I had no idea how many different factions existed within the walls of the city. I eyed the area by the car closest to the fence and took my chances at moving to it. My heart sank as I heard one of them speak.

"Did you guys hear that? I think someone is skulking around."

Their chatter turned into concerned whispering. I increased my pace to get behind the car. There was a gate to the right of its back end, and I assumed that's where they would come out of. This was bad already. My back was totally exposed and I could be surrounded by raiders at any moment. The people within went completely silent before I heard the gate swing open. The light of the fire cast a beam of radiance outside its opening and in the middle stood a shadow. I could tell it was holding a gun of some sort. I quietly inched my way around to the front of the car as I heard footsteps approaching.

"Hey! Someone's been over here! Listening in on us!", I heard a man shout out to his comrades.

"Should we get Glaive?", I heard another one say.

"Screw Glaive! We can handle this on our own! Probably just a little rat wandering around from another district".

He was coming around. I had to do something. I couldn't just surprise him and kill him... his friends would hear the altercation and flood outside, and who knew how many were in there. I rapidly scanned the ground for something. I found a heavily crushed can and picked it up. I gripped it tight and closed my eyes for a split second.

"Please. Please.", I whispered as softly as I could and winged the can at a nearby dumpster. I held my breath as a large man with a hole in his right cheek ran past.

"Where the hell are you ya little pig?", he snarled.

I was panicking. There was no way I could pull this off. I was insane. I followed him into the darkness by the dumpster. He hadn't heard me sneaking up on him. I was low to the ground, and being half his size, I knew he wouldn't spot me right away. I stood up silently and with all my might brought the sharp point on my giant wooden shiv into the right side of his neck. It punctured his skin and dug in as warm blood began rushing out of the wound. I must have stabbed deep, puncturing his larynx, because no scream emanated from his body. He gurgled and gasped as he swung around. I had ducked in behind the dumpster. He never saw me. I was shaking. I felt sick. I felt the thunderous boom of his body collapsing. A pool of blood grew quickly around his head.

    I could barely pick up the gun I was shaking so violently. I ran off as far from the fenced area as I could without being spotted. I made it to an alleyway where I hid behind another dumpster. I keeled over and began throwing up. I had never taken a life before. At least not to the extent that my memory would allow. After I had finished heaving, I wiped my mouth on my sleeve and looked down at the gun I had acquired. I opened its chamber and noticed that there were three shots loaded in.

    "Dammit! Why didn't I look for extra ammo?", I asked myself a little critically. I knew it couldn't be long until they alerted this 'Glaive' guy. After that, I'm sure their whole faction would be looking for the culprit. I'm sure they would just blame it on a rival group, but I didn't want to stick around to find out. I spotted a building and quietly made my way inside. Here, at least for the moment, I could breathe comfortably.

Chapter 15- The Other Side of Solace

Zephyr Apherius- 24

I had awoken in the cool, and damp cave. I had rappelled all the way down. Today I would be making my way across the bottom of the canyon and undertake the perilous journey back up the other side. I had been fortunate to keep myself out of trouble. I was extremely worried about the drop process. I had managed to get a bundle of tanks and my bike down to the bottom. These tanks would be enough to last me till I reached the top of the other side. I'd have a couple to spare if there were no errors or setbacks along the way. I was hoping that I would be fortuitous enough to find water in the caves on the other side. I stretched and looked around the tiny dugout and made my way over to the water trap. I dipped in and swam under, coming up on the other side. There, I had my supply pack. I slugged it over my shoulders and made my way out towards the rising sun. I figured I'd be completely dry again in an hour or so. I could see my bike at the bottom. It was very close. I was in a safe- zone, so to speak. Raiders rarely made it down here. That didn't take away from the eerie vibe it gave off, however. The place was essentially a massive graveyard. Corpses displaying various levels of decay lined the path on either side. Unfortunate souls who lost their balance or were forced down here by captors. The sound of the wind cutting through sounded like thousands of tormented souls. If it weren't for the sunlight, the combination of the two would surely drive me insane. I felt privileged to not have to be out on the canyon floor after dark.

Traversing my way up the other side would be a feat in itself. I initiated my descent.

I had that strange dream again. That man, Llaric Ephyon whose name wrote itself over my father's, approached me. I still harbored no fear as he silently took over my Father's memory. I hadn't ever seen him before, at least as far as I knew. He kept calling me Ophelia. Had I suppressed something in my past? Did it have some sort of meaning? I felt as though it were a betrayal of my father. Theodore Apherius was married to his work, and I never got to see much of him. I cherished the time we did have as he was always the upstanding parent when we were together. Perhaps his memory was so easily overwritten because his existence was too. He never enjoyed discussing work matters. There were even certain instances where he was prohibited from sharing information with us. I tried my best to hold on to every moment, and for the most part, him not discussing work was never a bother...

Until one day, he didn't come home.

That was the night I began seeing the Umbra. It stared at me with lifeless eyes. Almost as if it was looking through me. The maddening whispers always grew to unbearable decibels until I had no choice but to scream.

Why wouldn't he come home?

I remembered the Overseers had dispatched a car full of their special forces operatives to inform my mother of his disappearance. They were called the 'Phantom Ravens', and from the moment I had seen them, I knew that something wasn't quite right. I didn't feel they gave us all the information regarding his disappearance. After the report, my mother was out almost daily. Thinking back now I imagine that she was attempting to seek

council with the head researcher of my father's lab. Her exploits would always come up fruitless and she would return home in an aloof sort of state. She hadn't paid much attention to me after Dad was gone. The police were too busy back then, dealing with the supposed threat of the Vyridia. I knew that as a child, there was nothing I could do, however as I grew I came to understand the line of work my father was in a little better. Being in the Bios- Alpha facility had afforded me one memory that I thought I had lost ages ago. A name.
Printed in bold black text on the documents Katya and I had located. The name that signed off on every disgusting and inhumane project. The name that appeared just above my father's days before his disappearance. The name that would hold all the reasons he had to be taken from me.

Dr. Len Corvus...

Of course, many years had passed. Who knows what fate could have befallen such a heinous man. I hoped he was dead. I hoped he was rotting for the hell he put those innocent people through.

I had reached the cliff face with two oxygen tanks on my back. I swung my pick "CHCK" and again "CHCK". Every swing ingraining hatred into my head and adrenaline through my blood.

Why would no one tell me where the hell he was?! Why would Bios- Alpha cover up the fact that he had gone missing? They killed him! Oh God did they kill him? Did he learn too much....? Or maybe he let something slip in passing. They couldn't...
They wouldn't. Did those cowards kill my father?

A tear had made its way halfway down my cheek before I noticed I hadn't been moving. My arms had grown incredibly tired. I looked down and saw that the ground had all but disappeared. I shook myself from my thoughts and returned to a calm state of mind. The adrenaline rush was helpful but I would only tire my muscles further if I allowed it to continue. I began taking in large, slow breaths. I couldn't very well find the knowledge I sought if I was dead after all. I pressed upwards. closer I grew to the proverbial heavens. The sun was scorching like nothing I had ever felt before. I had to move quickly. I wouldn't be able to maintain my grip for much longer. I ascended as swiftly as I could. The cliff face felt as if it was going to continue into eternity. I had only one choice. Move. I miraculously brought my limbs back to life and began moving upwards. Fatigue hit me straight away but I kept pushing through. Flashes of Bios-Alpha kept crossing my mind. I felt as if I had forgotten something. I shook the images from my mind. I couldn't lose focus again. The edge of the cliff face was now visible! I cascaded into a feeling of bliss. I moved quicker than I ever had before, it was a little alarming actually. As my left hand reached the flat ground I began laughing. Covered in dirt and dust I pulled my body up to the top of the cliff. An open-mouthed smile shone through heavy breaths. In the distance, I could see the top of a city. The base of it was blurred out by sizzling heat. I took a sip from my canteen and pressed forward. I couldn't start my dugout too far from the canyon. I still had to rappel the other tanks up from the bottom and if I strayed too far, I could run out before I reached my destination. I turned around and looked back to the side I came from. It looked a lot further than I had previously anticipated. I owed the success to idle thought. Though the memories were painful, they made the trip across seem less taxing. A bead of sweat trickled down my brow before falling to the endless yellow beneath my feet. I looked once again to the sky and pondered how the Shift could have happened. Something I often did. I had no idea if anywhere in this barren world could sustain plant life anymore. I began digging as my pondering continued. I had once again lost myself in thought. When I next pulled myself out of it, the hole I had started was complete. The blistering sun was now a fading memory, disappearing in a red-orange glow. A crisp breeze blew through the desert whipping up sand particles. How refreshing. Perhaps not everything was all bad. Even in the vast expanse of the wastes that could drive anyone mad with its monotonous setting. Where every direction you looked, all you saw was the bland yellow sand, as if you were stuck in a snow globe. For me, I saw, clearly as the day, which direction I wanted to head. I elected to scout ahead for future dugouts and with a sudden confidence in my heart, I took in every angle of the wastes and laughed at them. Something good was going to come of this calamity. I could feel it in my bones. For the first time in a while, I felt as if nothing could get to me. The Umbra, the loss of my father or Kash, and the dreams I had been having about that strange man, Llaric Ephyon... None of it phased me at that moment. None of it mattered because, for the first time, I had direction! Come sunrise, I would be headed into my future.

Valian Sorik- 29

My eyes had grown immensely bloodshot. I had been staring at this computer screen for an endless eternity and I felt as though I could hear time itself ticking away in my head. Shredding pieces of my sanity away with its ferocious mandibles and carrying it off to the ceaseless nothing. The sound of Katya's voice snapped me back to reality.
    "You look like a damn zombie, Valian. Why don't you get some sleep?"
Her cheeky demeanor dragged me completely out of repose. That coy smile of hers always caught me off guard. She continued after I managed to bring my surely dopey expression to her.
    "I have something you're gonna wanna see", she added, beckoning me with a condescending finger.

She had brought me over to a blueprint she had been drawing up. She pointed out three large circles.
    "What am I looking at?", I inquired as I widened my eyes and rubbed them.

"These are ventilation ducts. Seems pretty normal right? Well, I found where they are situated, and they are graded for industrial purposes."

"What's your point, Kat?", I said with more than a hint of discombobulation.

"My point, Valian, is that there is no way in hell that an office space of this size would need ventilation of that caliber. Even with the giant oxygen bomb strapped to the back of it, this facility would maybe only require one of these systems. I have pinpointed at least three so far. This mega-system is feeding something much bigger, and I have reason to believe it's below us." She slowly brought her arm in front of her and extended her index finger towards the ground.

She said I was the one that needed sleep? She had clearly been drumming up conspiracies again. Although I had to admit, it made sense what she was saying. Why would Bios-Alpha need ventilation ducts of this size for a less- than substantial office space and a room housing a colossal oxygen tank.

"Did you find anything else on that Soros guy?", she prodded.

"Not much, honestly. He seemed rather keen on keeping his life private in all sectors. There isn't much data on him, but I did find something else that was a mite intriguing. A man by the name of Theodore Apherius...".
I could see the gears whirring in Katya's brain. She knew exactly who that name bore a synonymous nature to.

"Zephyr...". She barely choked out her name. It looked as though the realization winded her.

"The rabbit hole goes deeper", I continued. "You know how we found the list of agents and their vitals?"

She encouraged me with a nod and suspenseful stare.

"The day one Theodore Apherius' vitals went grey was 11.27.2534. The very same day that test subject successfully integrated with that... that- thing. You know, the top-secret project you and Zeph were looking at. Project-".

"Glass Shadow", Katya said with a small tremor in her voice. Her eyes were looking past me to the filing cabinets. I could see tears welling up in her sad, blue eyes.

"It was right in front of us the whole time... FUCK!" Katya jumped up and cast her blueprints of the makeshift table where they were resting.

"For years she kept this inside! She never bothered anyone with the loss of her father! Now we find out its been in this dusty old computer graveyard staring us right in the fucking face?! Mocking us?! TOYING WITH HER!!"
I jumped up and grabbed her into a tight hug.

"They paid, Katya. They paid for the horrors they imposed."

"How could they just rip a little girl away from her family like that? Just erase her father in a meaningless failure of a test? It's not fair... She left before we could tell her."
I remained quiet as I attempted to console Katya. I didn't think it right to inform Zephyr of the nature of her Father's death as I had no actual proof that he was the subject submitted to those tests. The dates could purely be a coincidence, but I didn't want to rile up Katya more than she already was so I kept my mouth shut and listened to the blade-like sobs that sliced through the silence with every manifestation. It hurt me too. To think someone could have done this to our friend. Our sister. Zephyr deserved an explanation. An explanation that would likely never be answered. On the long- shot that anyone from Eclypse was still around, I highly doubt they'd be willing to speak with us. Still, I could feel an anger welling up inside of me that could only be repressed by a satisfactory answer.
Did those bastards kill Zephyr's father? Could she already have these questions running through her head? I hoped to god that the calamity took their lives and made them suffer. I wouldn't allow this world to harbor such vile beasts. I was going to figure out what they were hiding in the basement of this facility, and when I did, I

was going to destroy anyone who had attached their names to these putrid experiments.

Katya Malikov- 25

    The deep-seated hatred I harbored for these people was stronger than the immeasurable force of a tidal wave... and I had not even met a single one of them. It was like a feeling of vitriol towards the ghosts of a memory that didn't even belong to me. I felt I owed it to Zephyr to take on her share of anger as well, considering she couldn't be here to bear her portion. What the hell went on here? It was like a fucking synthetic doomsday. I felt my chest heaving with breaths of pure rage. I could feel my fingernails digging into Valian as he attempted to face my divine rage alone. Not once did he wince or groan. He just held it all in. Caging the monster that was crawling out from every pore of my body. I knew right then and there that some sort of unspoken agreement had been made. We would eliminate any one of those Bios- Alpha scumbags that still had the audacity to live after the things they had done. As my breathing shallowed, I felt Valian's grip on me loosen and I was finally able to look around the room and see the physical manifestation of my virulence. Valian placed his thumb and forefinger on my chin, the entire time he said nothing. He stared directly into my eyes, freezing all time around us before letting go and walking past me to clean up. My entire world had settled into a dead calm. Words weren't needed for the powerful energy that had just blanketed this condemned shithole of an office.

    I knew this wasn't only for Zephyr but for Kash too. Though even he was a heavy loss to her. If anyone took anything else from her, I wouldn't hesitate to erase everything that they loved before watching the life drain from their eyes. I let out one final deep breath before the malicious thoughts were able to rest within me once again.

The time was coming to restock Zephyr on her provisions, but first, Valian and I had a primary mission. Elucidating the destination of the ventilation systems within this compound. We planned to head back to old HQ and return with a high-intensity torch that had the capability to cut through anything in this place. After all, if you can't uncover secrets the conventional way, you could always melt the things obscuring them instead.

Chapter 16- Glaive

Llaric Ephyon- 35

    The frigid stone that I rested my back upon offered little to no comfort over the shouting of oncoming raiders. My clothing was dingy and mangled from a combination of the sand I had kicked up on my bike as well as my manoeuvers over the rubble of the lost city. My make-shift shank was stained with blood that had since soaked into the wood I had made it from. The blood that my weapon hadn't gorged itself on had made its way down to my fingers which were a dead white. I had been gripping it as tightly as possible since I set foot in Malvora. It was a symbol of my survival and to let it go would be to let go of my very life.

    The shouting grew nearer. The raiders were in heavy numbers and I had no idea how many factions had joined the search to find the little rat that had managed to skulk its way onto their turf. I silently made my way upstairs and quietly entered one of the few intact suites that remained in the building. I was greeted with an odd sight.
 Most residences were abandoned in swift haste and left virtually untouched in the wake of Eclypse's tirade through the streets. However, this suite I was in was practically empty, aside from a few destroyed computers. The layers of dust almost rendered them indescribable. Someone had been squatting here. I was trapped in a time capsule. The lack of furnishing and the destroyed computers completely overtaken by dust led me to the conclusion that this was once a hide-out for Vyridia victims. How long had it been left in this condition? A bat rested neatly against the corner of the wall closest to the smashed computers. In contrast to the yellowing paint, the bat looked more or less ageless, like time had

not worn away at it. No rust or even dents to speak of. It even managed to stave off the years of dust that had settled on everything else. I scoured the suite and located a small list of food items in one of the cupboards. It was scrawled rather hastily which further solidified to me that this place was once inhabited by squatters. I could glean nothing more from the barren apartment. I quietly made my way out of the suite and back down the stairs, passing the occasional blown-out hole in the wall.

After checking a few other suites, I came to the conclusion that there was no source of food within. The festering thought I had growing in the back of my mind loomed over me. The only place I would be able to find any sort of sustenance would be in a raider encampment. Sneaking into one would be no easy task, and getting back out with all the food would be even more difficult. It wouldn't be efficient to utilize the shank much longer. What other choice did I have, though? I weighed my options carefully and concluded that attempting the heist was my best option for survival... As a matter of fact, it was the only option that held any potential for survival. I could easily turn around, head home, and let starvation overtake me, but that would mean undoing everything I had worked so hard to preserve. I knew I had to risk it. I took one final sweep of the floor before taking my leave. The insipid rooms brought me back to a time where I had lived in Malvora, completely carefree. I had no idea how bad the poorer classes had it. The monotony of the rooms was only the tip of an otherwise mountainous iceberg. The structural integrity was precarious, to say the least. And the smell of mold and mildew lingered in the air, threatening its stability further. The presence of raiders sure didn't help their case either. They weren't exactly the pinnacle of caring and many buildings had succumbed to their demise much like this one was about to. I cautiously descended the stairs. I had given no thought as to whether or not there might be raiders calling this teetering death trap home. As I quietly receded from the front of the building, I saw a harshly degraded sign that once welcomed its residents. "Presta Apartments. Welcome home!" As I read I was interrupted by the sound of nearby shouting. I was lucky that the raiders were loud. I'd have been found out by now. I ducked behind a pillar awaiting them to pass, but they seemed keen on continuing their discussion right around the corner. It wasn't hard to eavesdrop on their conversation. Not that I was able to do anything until they elected to finish up.

"Scouts sayin' that Otherworlder is coming through town." I heard one of them spew.

"She ain't takin our city if that's what you're worried about. We got Glaive after all. He has them fancy abilities, what'll scare her outta town", loudly responded the other.

"I mean havin' a Vyridia in the place kinda boosts morale, but the scouts were sayin' that she might be a threat to him."

"You're worryin' about nothin'. Who knows, maybe she's a pretty little thing. We could always show her a little Malvora... hospitality". I felt my face contort in disgust as their greasy laughter echoed around the corner tainting anything in earshot.

"Well, now I'm hoping she comes through".

The laughter continued but this time it was drifting away. They were on the move. I poked my head around the corner and scouted my next option. A well-hidden doorway leading to a basement was across the square. All I had to do was make it there. I took in a few rapid breaths and as I took off towards the door I held on to the last one for a second. I looked around in darting glances. I was in the clear. I approached the steps leading down. As I reached for the door, I was greeted with a sharp stinging pain in the neck. I reached towards the source and to my surprise, a dart had been lodged beneath my skin. As my vision darkened, I noticed a well-camouflaged individual with a blowgun staring at me, completely bewildered. In their eyes, I saw bolstered fear and rage. Then, for the first time in a while, I slept without consequence. No cryptic beings with fountains of unyielding knowledge. No prophecies. Just... blissful silence.

I finally awoke to the sound of disjointed chatter and the flickering light of a raging fire. I appeared to be housed in a tent of sorts. As my vision slowly adjusted itself, I made an attempt to move and found that I had been bound. My wrists were burning and on the cusp of going numb. I gritted my teeth as a voice addressed me. It was gruff and unpleasant. The smell of cigarette smoke wafted close by. Whoever it was was near.

"You got some balls showing up here, Rat. I'd be torturing you, right now myself if I didn't have orders"

My vision had come into full focus and I could see my captor. He was a rather bulky fellow. His right eye was glazed over. It was evident he had sustained some damage to it. It was almost difficult to make out the scar on his forehead through his greasy unkempt hair. The smoke I had smelled earlier was emanating from a cigarette that had burned almost down to the filter. It hung out the end of the man's angry scowl as he scrutinized me. His next words trailed after the toxic smog jetting from his nose.

"Glaive wanted to see you personally. Must be some sort of special case. Consider yourself lucky".

He flicked the end of his cigarette at me and with a sharp exhale exited the tent.

Another voice directed itself at me. I deduced that it had to have been who the first man was talking to. As he spoke, the loud high pitched 'zing' of a large blade being sharpened was heard. A sword or a scythe for sure.

"Don't try anything. I've been given the order to incapacitate you should you try and run".

The large sickle-blade came down in front of me making land between my sprawled out knees. I let out a loud yell and began breathing rapidly. As it stood in the ground in front of me I could make out all the features of the scythe. It looked to be custom made and within the intricacies of its artwork, I could tell it was rather weathered. I knew he would likely be extremely proficient with this weapon, and elected to heed his word. As he walked into view, he seemed rather out of place for a raider. He was clean and dressed in somewhat fashionable clothing. The strangest thing was that his eyes were entirely shielded by a white wrap of some sort. I remained silent. It was peculiar. Aside from the ceaseless adrenaline rush, I had experienced no fear. Something told me that the individual before me had no malicious intent behind their actions.

"Who are you?", I asked seemingly involuntarily. He did not respond. I decided not to push my luck with questioning and silently waited for my potential demise. It was funny. I swore that I could hear the ticking of a clock piercing the dead silence. The idea of time always had a way of sneaking into my psyche when I was at my lowest points. I found that no matter how often I cursed the name of time, its concept still pushed me to survive. To persevere.

"Have you seen it?" I asked the man with the eye wraps.
"What are you talking about?", he replied calmly.
"The Umbra"
He made a short panicked sound. Bingo. His reaction told me two things.
One was that he knew of the creature I was speaking of, and two that he knew Zepher Apherius. I continued my questioning.

"Where can I find her? The Apherius girl."
"I- I have no idea what you mean." He stammered. He was frightened. Something I never thought was possible. Just seconds ago he stood so stoic I could have sworn he was nothing more than a statue. I was fairly certain I knew something.
"Zephyr Apherius was the one who came up with the name for the creature. I think you know that, and I speculate that the creature is why you have removed your eyes. Am I right?"
His breathing increased. I heard the metal swing of his blade. Had I gone too far? Either way, something traumatizing happened to this man, and it had something to do with the Umbra and this Apherius woman. I would get the information I sought.

"Shut your damn mouth, Rat!". The blade stopped inches from my temple.

I cast my gaze upward and saw that his efforts had been thwarted by a mere child.

"Now now, Yoma. There's no need to be so hostile towards our guest. How am I to question him if you leave him without a head, hmm?"

The boy seemed intelligent beyond his years. He looked no more than 12 years of age, yet he spoke with the cold calculation of a war tactician. He looked down at me with a wildly inhuman expression. The first feature that caught my attention was the presence of heterochromia in his eyes... a distinctive trait of the Vyridia back then.

"So... you have decided to take from us. A very unfortunate thing, I must say."

His aura was heavy. It felt like I was once again being asphyxiated by the sheer vastness of despair.

"What was your end game? Did you really think that you would be able to pull it off?"

"I'm just hungry", I said desperately.

"You're just hungry? Let me ask you something. Do you know what they used to do back in the day when someone was caught stealing?"

I knew the kinds of atrocities that were committed in the days of old, yet for some reason, I still shook my head in silence as if to prolong the pain I was about to experience.

"Well", he began "First, they would tie down the offender at the arms, so as to prevent any squirming. Then a sharp implement such as..."

He stopped as he scanned the room for a second and grabbed Yoma's scythe.

"...this would be used to remove said offender's hands."

Everything in the child's face was not unlike cold, emotionless stone.

"They call me Glaive around here, what is your name criminal?"

I stared into his eyes and answered slowly.
"Llaric Ephyon"
His eyes widened and he stumbled back.
The one he called Yoma looked over in my direction.
"Interesting", I heard him mumble.
Glaive spoke up as he looked around the room in an almost panicked state.
"Dismemberment is too good for this one. Keep him here until I can sort out an ample punishment for his heinous acts."
In one swift motion, he swung his leg across my face. The room spun as I felt the heat of the blood dripping out of my mouth. He then spun around and exited the tent. The familiar flicking of Vyridia wings followed him out. I was puzzled, to say the least. Yoma sauntered over to his scythe that now lay prone on the ground. A sickening smile painted across his face.
"How fascinating! I never thought you of all people would have survived. Fate really is mysterious". He commenced in a disjointed cackle that one would expect to hear from a patient in a psych ward. It left me feeling greater unease than the prospect of losing my hands. His cackling continued as he exited the tent, leaving me alone. I spit blood into the dirt below me as I stared after him.

Chapter 17- Her Secrets

???- ???

I surveyed the state he was in. The sinking feeling in the pit of my stomach told me that something needed to be done. There was something bothering me, however. Why was it that he hadn't struggled once since his capture? That strange man brought his scythe down precariously close to Mr. Ephyon's legs. That would be enough to make even those with the strongest resolve jump in terror. I spun around and saw that the Seraphim was watching with me. I cast my gaze down as the sinking feeling grew.
"There's nothing we can do... is there?"
The same smile that always adorned her face remained. Even though she always had half of it covered I could always feel the full weight of the emotions ruminating from her. She responded without hesitation in a calming tone
"There is nothing we are meant to do, my dear child".
I turned back to watch the events unfold. The Seraphim continued speaking.
"You remember why Mr. Ephyon is special, yes?"
I nodded in silence as I watched him look around the tent.
"Then you understand why it is imperative that we mustn't interfere with his growth. Any losses he succumbs to are meant to help him flourish."
I let out a long breath, longing for his freedom. Both from captivity as well as the shackles that bogged him down in his reality. I hoped with all my might that she would show up in time. Seraphim spoke once more before taking her leave.
"All will be as it should". I had wondered what her origins entailed. What had she gone through to remain so calm and collected through the turmoils she faced as the Seraphim. Hopelessness

was the name given to her, and it was one that she seemingly cherished. I knew that she, like Valiance, was from a time before time itself. I knew that her ancient inner workings must have been what prepared her for the role she had undertaken. Yet I couldn't help but feel that the throes of sorrow were beyond burdensome for someone so old. She was deserving of a name much more grandiose than Hopelessness. I just couldn't understand. Why had I been selected to become her successor? What was so special about me? Perhaps in time, I would see the direction that the winds of fate were blowing. For now, though, it was apparent I was being kept in the dark about something. I knew my time would come to learn this secret, and until then I voted to feign curiosity. I suppose that was my duty as her apprentice.

Chapter 18- Beneath The Surface

Katya Malikov- 25

I had awoken rather early. Just as I had when Zephyr left. After today I would be heading to resupply her and I had no indication of how she was getting on. I had no idea what I was going to find. I was a bundle of nerves, to say the least, but I had to trust she was okay. I took solace in the fact that she wouldn't go down without a fight, but I also still possessed the residual shock of the news I had learned earlier. I couldn't help but wonder if the news of her father would be the fight that does bring her down... then it would be by my hand that she would break. It killed me to think about, but she deserved to know. There wasn't much left on this mortal coil to protect, but she and Valian were the only ones I absolutely refused to let down. I rose from my sleeping bag and looked over to where Valian usually rested and I noticed he was absent. The abnormally shaped lump even through the darkness of the office was clearly not a person. I rubbed the sleep from my eyes and made my way over to the sink. I turned the tap and placed my cupped hands below the now steady stream of water. As I drank it, I was interrupted by a rather loud snapping sound followed by a disgruntled series of curse words courtesy of Valian. He had been picking the place apart slowly to find out why the facility needed three enormous ventilation systems. I laughed quietly as I made my way to the source of the noise. I rounded a corner towards the back of the facility. Valian had ripped down a wall panel that revealed a small room. The panel looked as though it were once on hinges that could be swung open. However, after Valian's

tirade on it, that would no longer be the case. It was funny thinking of how much effort he put in to remove a door that could have just been opened normally. I stepped through the miniature chaos he had created and saw him standing over a hatch with innumerable crowbars stuck into its seams. His arms were crossed. He looked dirty and defeated as he cast a glance up at me and made a motion towards the hatch.
"It's not playing nice," he said.
"Well that's because it's a door, not an acupuncture patient"
Valian looked back down at the hatch
"You hear that?! Katya knows what you are! You're in trouble now!"
I approached the hatch and scoured it for a minute. I then directed my attention to a panel on the wall. I mouthed the word "bingo" to Valian as he sent me a sour look. Pulling one of his many crowbars, I skipped jovially over to the wall panel and popped the faceplate off. A smattering of wires fell out and I began shuffling through them. I found the one sending electricity to the hatch's locking mechanism and snipped it with a pair of nearby shears. The hatch unlocked with a confident pop. I could hear Valian let out a long sigh behind me. It brought a smile to my face and before I knew it I was laughing. I could hear Valian erupting into fits as well. It was nice to have moments like this. Moments that temporarily abated the all-too-familiar crushing vices of despair.

As our laughter died down, we re-aligned our focus on the hatch. Someone had been hiding something. I was thinking it was likely the crackpot who ran this facility back in the day. That same brute who I believed was responsible for the death of Zephyr's father. Valian and I slowly lifted the hatch together. It belted a loud creak as it slowly revealed its contents to us.
There was a ladder leading down into a dark, sightless pit. It was rather perturbing, but I knew right away that whatever was down there was the answer to our questions. Valian descended the ladder into the swallowing abyss. I lowered myself down after him

and was greeted by the overwhelming darkness as well. As I looked around I saw a few small green and red lights as they cut through the blackness. Before I could approach them, the entire room became enshrouded in light. I spun around and saw Valian at a panel of switches.

"Found the lights", he said sheepishly. I retorted with an overly animated thumbs up before having a look around the room. To call it a room would be an understatement. It looked like we were in a fully functional laboratory. Everything looked ominously clean for being abandoned this long. Numerous offices lined the hallways at the far end. I felt a twinge of anger as I knew what kinds of things I might find in one of the aforementioned offices. As I made my way over I looked into numerous chambers blocked off by glass. One, in particular, had caught my attention as it appeared to be sealed off with thick metal walls. Danger tape was strewn haphazardly across it with a message taped over it.

"This testing chamber is suspended indefinitely. Use of this chamber is strictly forbidden.

-Lumis Goodwill, Head of Theta Sector"

The note was perplexing, to say the least. I had my theories as to what could have put this particular chamber into indefinite lockdown, but couldn't say for sure. Furthermore, the locking mechanisms for the door were a complex manual system that required numerous keys to unlock. With a warning of this magnitude, I could only suspect that the keys were taken when this facility was abandoned so that no one could stumble upon it and let their curiosity get the better of them.
As I continued walking, something prevented me from breaking eye contact with this chamber for a moment. Something was obviously wrong, and I was wondering if whatever was in there was still dangerous.

I approached the offices hesitantly. I pushed the open door to the first one and with a loud creaking sound I could see fully inside. The nameplate on the desk read "Dr. Cohen Sayah". Undoubtedly one of Len Corvus' associates. I could feel the adrenaline flow through my veins like an unbridled tempest. A crawling, sickly feeling soon followed and I searched the neatly kept office for any signs of malpractice or anything that could lead me to the reason Zephyr's father had to die. I walked over to the desk and booted up the computer. To my surprise, it wasn't password protected. Likely because the doctors here never anticipated anyone finding their lab. I opened up Dr. Sayah's emails and began looking. One of them was the same one we read upstairs that was broadcasted to all of Bios-Alpha, however, I noticed something that we had previously missed. An additional recipient that received this particular email. The tag read "DRAIDA Mainframe". I knew that Bios-Alpha had dealings with DRAIDA, but I had only surmised that DRAIDA was offering defense protocols to this facility. My hypothesis was smashed as I further explored Dr. Sayah's emails. It would appear that Bios-Alpha would take contracts from DRAIDA and perform these heinous experiments at their behest. It seemed like Bios-Alpha was just a puppet. Perhaps I had been directing my rage at the wrong person. Something still didn't seem right. I clicked the search bar in Dr. Sayah's email and typed in 'Glass Shadow'. Surely enough, a couple of results popped up on the screen and DRAIDA was labeled as the primary sender. One of them was also labeled with the name Daynon Soros, the chairman of Bios-Alpha. The subject line was labeled 'Project Failure and Termination'. I opened the email to see if any of the contents could shine some light on the questions I had been harboring.

From: DRAIDA Mainframe; Dr. Daynon Soros

To: Dr. Cohen Sayah

CC: Dr. Len Corvus

To Theta Sector Team

This email is to outline the termination of Project Glass Shadow. The previously mentioned casualties as a result of project contamination have marked Glass Shadow as a failure.

The negligent acts of your sector have resulted in the loss of life and the potential release of the deadly 'Scourge' material into the world.

We at DRAIDA, alongside Bios- Alpha Chair, Dr. Daynon Soros have agreed that this incompetence cannot go unpunished. It has been declared that your facility will be shut down. Any future practices henceforth shall be criminalized. In accordance with Malvoran law, you are all subject to questioning pertaining to the death of one Dr. Theodore Apherius.

A call has also been made between Dr. Soros and the administration at DRAIDA to forbid Dr. Len Corvus from engaging in any kind of scientific practice. All licenses have been permanently suspended.

Best of Luck,

Aya Rahnbyo

CEO; DRAIDA Corp.

Daynon Soros

Chairman; Bios- Alpha

The words in the email reverberated off the walls in my head. All my speculations were correct. I felt sick to my stomach. The death of Zephyr's father had been sitting under our noses this entire time. I knew it from the evidence I had discovered upstairs, but this email had been the confirmation that I sought. I also believed I knew why that chamber was cordoned off with metal walls and danger tape. It would also appear that Upon Dr. Corvus' termination, Lumis Goodwill took over and continued the operation of the Theta sector in silence. I solemnly shut down the computer and left the office.

How could they? How could they rip a little girl away from the only family she had left?

The next office was empty and disturbingly enough, there was no trace of a Dr. Theodore Apherius ever existing at Theta Sector.

My heart broke for Zephyr. The empty office that likely once contained all of his things, was gone. There wasn't anything I could grab for her and I highly doubt an email outlining his death would bring her any comfort. I was lost and baffled as to how anyone could do something like this. My macabre trance was shattered by the sound of Valian's voice

"One hell of a place, hey?" he said with a half-cocked smile.

"Oh yeah. It's definitely hell", I replied, still half-aloof.

"So I found something you're gonna want to see"

The statement aroused my curiosity as I followed him out of the office area. We rounded a rather small corner that led to a large carpeted section of the lab. Before us, stood a giant vault door.

"Oh joy", I started. "Another one"

"This door is impossibly complex. It's entirely custom made so there are no algorithms I can work off of to try and hack it. I'm just gonna have to figure out the passcode. That is if this thing still even works."

I had far too much on my mind to ponder the contents of that vault. I was confident I would like what we found in there anyway. It was entirely too much.

"Hey Val, you got a cigarette?", I asked. "I need some air".

He shot me a quizzical look, but shrugged it off and procured a perfectly intact cigarette out of his jacket.

"Mind if I join ya?"

I smiled at him before responding

"Topside we go"

We left the lights on in the laboratory. It's not like anyone was collecting bill payments anymore anyway. We climbed the ladder and made our way outside to the orange glow of the sun as it beat down on the place of a thousand secrets. I hadn't craved a cigarette in quite some time. Valian handed me a lighter that was caked with dirt. When you found things in the wastes, you tended to cherish them no matter the condition they were in. Odds are you wouldn't come across another lighter, or knife in the desert. As I lit the end of the cigarette, the glow of the morning sun encapsulated it. The smoke rising off of it, disappearing into oblivion above me. I wondered how Zephyr was faring, completely oblivious to the mountain of intel I had uncovered in the lab. Of course, she had more pressing things to tend to. Her journey was harrowing, that I knew. To trek endlessly through the desert and across a monolithic canyon in hopes of finding something that may not even be there, was an undertaking that required no less than the purest resolve. I was confident that she would be unbothered by her escapade. The one bit of solace I seemingly had left.

I held out hope that I could bring her back home, where she could be safe with Valian and me. Though in this world of uncertainty, this world of violence, who really knew what could be taken away in the blink of an eye?

Chapter 19- The Otherworlder

Llaric Ephyon- 35

I awoke to the sounds of shouting. From what I could tell, it was an altercation between Glaive and Yoma. I squinted as my eyes adjusted to the new light that was now pouring through the fibers of the tent I was held in. My arms and back were sore from the position I had been tied in. It was a wonder that I had even been able to sleep. Hunger pounded against my stomach like a caged beast trying to free itself. I had to eat something. The urge was unbearable. I looked around the room for something to cut my binds. I knew that It would be difficult as I was tied to the anchoring post of the tent. As I scoured around, Yoma returned to me, a grimace painted across his visage.

"Rough day at the office?" I pestered.

"I've never seen you wear a sense of humor, Ephyon. How annoying"

"Doesn't look like you're seeing much of anything these days"

He spun around and I could feel his gaze on me through sightless eye sockets.

"You still don't remember me do you?", He asked before continuing.
"The only person I had ever looked up to. The only person who was able to understand my talents and forge a new frontier with

them. 'The Umbra' as you call it, took everything from me. It's all because of that bastard, Apherius!"

He stopped for a second before waving a suspecting finger in the air.

"It plagues you too, doesn't it, Ephyon? The creature? Why is it that you were permitted to keep your vision?"

"How did you know that I see it?" I asked

"All who have seen it are tied. Marked for death! We are the same now, Ephyon! Walking husks of our former selves. Oh! How's that daughter of yours?"

"What do you know about Ophelia?" I questioned getting rather heated.

"Well, at least you remember her. What a shame it would be... You're missing pieces, dear Brother. You can't complete a puzzle with missing pieces"

My growing rage had been misplaced. Whoever this was, was clearly a few screws short of a shed. His mind had been completely warped by the Umbra. I couldn't take anything he said too seriously. His actions from what I could tell were completely unpredictable.

"What I'm missing is breakfast. Is there any way you could be a pal and bring me something?"

Yoma began to chuckle. It grew into full-on maniacal laughter before he immediately silenced himself and spoke once more.

"Why not get searching?" He asked.

133

My confusion peaked as I heard the sound of metal hitting wood, immediately followed by the loosening of my hands as they fell to my side. It was apparent that Yoma had cut the binds. I looked at my hands before looking over at him.

"Time is running out. She will be here soon, and I want to see what you will do until then."

He erupted into another laughing fit while I reached down to where my feet were bound and began to untie the rest of myself.

"Who will be here soon?", I questioned

"The otherworlder. Another that you have met, yet may not know. Oh how exciting!", Yoma replied in jovial candor.

"Why are you helping me?"

"Without Yggdrasil, we fall"

My heart immediately began to race. I hadn't heard that phrase since my last encounter with the Umbra. I had no true inkling as to its meaning, but it followed me relentlessly. What were this man's true motives?

"If you see Glaive, you leave him to me." Yoma finished coldly.

I looked around the tent for a weapon and found a pistol that looked functional. I loaded it with a nearby clip and turned to the blind man one last time.

"Uh... Thanks, Yoma", I said

"Oh come now, that name is for clients! You and I are old friends, so you can just call me Len"

I looked him over for a second before leaving without another word. I was a sitting duck in a thriving raider encampment in broad daylight. Not ideal odds for my survival, but I had to satisfy my primitive urges or I wouldn't be able to realign myself with the task at hand...

Locating the Pillars of Light.

    I tried to keep myself tucked away in the shadows while I searched for food. I felt feral. Apart from myself. The animalistic feeling gave me a sense of invulnerability. I harbored less fear than I normally would in a situation such as this. I saw across the street, the silhouette of a man in a tent sitting down. I quietly approached, pistol drawn. I poked my head in through the tent flaps and saw that the man was throwing down mouthfuls of what appeared to be some sort of chowder. I removed my mask, took my anchor off my back, and set it down. I then took aim at him and fired. The bullet made contact with the back of his head. He slumped forward and blood began pouring from his wound. Surely the sound of gunfire would alert others to my position. I had to be fast. I approached his bowl that was still half full and began scarfing down the contents. It tasted dirty, but I didn't care. The wave of hunger was too powerful to pass anything up at this point. Warm, fresh blood soaked the sides of the bowl. I finished the nasty chowder, but the hunger had not subsided. I felt I was going insane. I remembered looking down at the man I had shot before completely blacking out. It was as if something took over my body and forced me into a stasis. I gazed into an endless pit of emptiness for what felt like hours. When my consciousness was restored to me, I was tucked behind yet another dumpster. My entire body was covered with a wet sensation. I looked down at my hands which were now completely covered in blood. My clothes were stained as well. Furthermore, I could feel a similar wetness around my mouth. My esperata was back on and the mask prevented the blood from drying to my face. The strangest part was that my hunger had completely subsided. I didn't want to think of what could have happened in those moments I lost.

      I pulled out my pistol and counted 7 remaining rounds. I had to leave this place. It appeared that my senses returned when my hunger disappeared. What a stupid idea this was. I was baffled that I wasn't dead or dismembered. The things that these raiders did to intruders were unspeakable. I had to leave, and the only way out was with a fight. There was no way I was going to be able to sneak through the whole city back to my bike. The time had come to pull myself up and make my way out. I made my way out to the sun-soaked square and began to head north where my bike was. I heard the sound of chatter as I approached the next street. Rusty signs creaking in the mid-day wind told me I was heading up Mechaline Avenue. Two raiders were blocking my path as I rounded the corner. They hadn't spotted me yet. I pulled out my pistol and shot one in the head. I fired a second time and hit the other raider in the shoulder. He yelled for help before ducking behind a building to arm himself. This was bad. I only had five rounds left and I didn't want to waste them on one guy. I could see three more coming in from the west. I tucked myself behind the building they were approaching, while also watching where the first raider I shot was. I heard the yelling grow closer as I leaned around the corner and shot the three raiders.
I still hadn't seen the one that disappeared behind the building adjacent to me. Had he bled out? I decided to rush him. He would suspect me to run headlong into gunfire. I raced across the street to where I had killed the first raider and rounded the corner with my gun pointed straight out in front of me. To my surprise, the hiding raider was nowhere to be seen. I ran down to the alleyway which was the only other available hiding place as the road he went down hit a dead end with an unscalable wall. After turning up

nothing, I returned to the main road where the group of three raiders had been situated. I could see one more hiding behind a derelict vehicle. I slowly made my way to approach him but was greeted by an immediate agonizing pain in my side.
I let out a pained yell. I instinctively made my way into a nearby gas station. I broke the windows locking me out and snuck inside. I hid in the cooler in the back and was finally able to inspect the pain I had just felt.

    Looking down to my right side I noticed a sizable arrow protruding from just below my bottom right rib. I crawled around searching the shelves for anything useful to help me. All I could find was an old washcloth tucked behind the cashier's area. I grabbed the arrow and with one hard pull, it dislodged itself from my body. The pain was immense. I immediately placed the cloth on my injury and pressed hard. I had no idea what to do. I only had 2 bullets left and I couldn't very well run back out to pick up another weapon lest I succumbed to another attack. If they decided to come look for me, it would be the end. I closed my eyes and let out a long breath as I pulled my anchor off my back once again to look at it. Its glow was fading much like my life force. I admired the dying flicker for a moment as I apologized to all those I had failed in my reckless pursuit of sustenance. I gently set the anchor down as it lay back against the cooler wall.

    I had never believed in miracles until this whole thing started. I had always felt doomed to fail. All I wanted was to protect Ophelia and give her some semblance of a normal life, but I couldn't even do that. However, I had vowed to myself not to fail her in this endeavor. Why had I been apologizing like I was giving up? I knew I couldn't give up. I needed to return to my reality. Then I could have the answers. Everything I needed to know about my daughter! I looked down at my anchor once more and noticed that the glow was returning, growing brighter and brighter. Its light now enveloped the entire cooler, almost blinding me. Then I heard

more shouting and gunfire. In a matter of seconds, it had faded leaving only one sound left. The calling of my name.
It was the sound of a woman's voice shouting from outside.

"Llaric Ephyon! Get your sorry ass out here!"

It was unfamiliar to me. It was anything I had heard in the camp before. Come to think of it, I don't think I had seen any women in the raider encampment who knew me by name. I slowly crawled to the door. I had nothing else to lose. I was fully aware this could be the thing that killed me, however even through her harsh bellowing, something coaxed me towards her. I managed to stand up and push open the gas station door and make my way outside to where I saw the source of the yelling.

Before me stood a woman with long blonde hair and rather peculiar-looking armor that I could only describe as some sort of fantasy military. In one hand she held a pistol and in the other an armament that matched her armor. It appeared to be some sort of celestial lance. Black wings flickered on her back. I managed to speak.

"Y-you're a... Vyrida"?

She looked over at me and looked almost annoyed.

"What the hell have you gotten yourself into, you idiot? Don't you realize you could be killed? Or perhaps you were aiming to have all of Daedalus' plans go up in smoke!" She yelled.

"I don't... who are you?", I inquired.

She gave me a puzzled look before continuing.

"Man, Lumis really did a number on you didn't he?"

Lumis... I had heard that name before... but where? How much of my memory had I truly lost? The strange woman continued.

"Look, I will explain everything to you once we get out of here. For now, we gotta move"

She pressed a finger to my arrow wound. It slowly began to close before my very eyes. Shocking as it was, I remained almost unphased by it. I had seen so many unexplainable things in recent times that I elected not to question it.

"Better?", she pressed.

"Uh yeah, thanks"

"Take this", she continued, handing me her pistol.

We began running towards an exit from the city. Raiders poured out and I began firing. One by one they dropped until a thunderous boom was heard, stopping everyone in their tracks. A figure on top of a nearby building began descending to the ground. It was Glaive. He had what appeared to be an electrically charged sword. His eyes were glowing white. All the surrounding raiders jumped behind any cover they could find. The woman who saved me seemed entirely unwavering against this personified force of nature.

"It's been a while, Faedesta Oburon", she said calmly. I looked over at her, in complete disbelief that she knew Glaive.

"You return to my domain to take what's rightfully mine! I cannot allow you to live for this transgression!"

I spoke to the woman once more.

"Do you think you can take him?", I asked

She didn't break eye contact with him as she responded to my inquiry.

"He's only a Vyridia, it would be a cakewalk fighting him, however, it is not my destiny in the tides of fate to engage in combat with him today. That role belongs to another as we make our escape".

"Okay... and who might that be?"

With her sights on Glaive still unfaltering, she pointed past me. I followed the direction of her finger and noticed Yoma running in towards us with that same sickly smile that he always wore.

"Him", replied the woman.

Glaive looked over at the fast-approaching Yoma.

"You fool Yoma! You would betray me?"

"Don't take it so personally, Oburon! You are merely an obstacle in the way of Daedalus!" Yoma replied, pulling back his scythe.

"You really hope to stand a chance against a Vyridia?" Glaive mocked.

"I've spent most of my life surrounded by them. Reading them. Examining their battle techniques. You won't be a problem!"

In the blink of an eye, Glaive had disappeared and reappeared in front of Yoma who had successfully parried Glaive's lightning-quick attack with the utmost ease.

"Better get going, Cygnus! Wouldn't want to keep him waiting", Yoma shouted!

The woman nodded at Yoma and turned to me.

"Let's go".

With that, she grabbed my arm and flew me out of the city with blinding speed. In a split second, we were over my pod in the desert. She gently landed and set me down.

"It's time to get back on track, Llaric.", she told me. "You need to compile the pieces missing in your memory. It is imperative to the final waves of fate."

"Great", I responded "More cryptic crap".

"Oh no, I'm not like that. Do you know how annoying it is to sit in on a meeting with the rest of Daedalus? No no. I'm going to tell you everything you need to know."

"Oh thank God" I choked.

She let out a laugh before inviting herself into my home.

"Come on, you're gonna want to sit down"

"Wait", I called after her.

She spun around to meet my gaze

"What's your name?"

"My name is Calio Cygnus. A Vaskyr in the employ of Daedalus. I also used to work with you some years back. Come on, let's have a chat"

Chapter 20- Missing Rendezvous

Zephyr Apherius- 24

    I didn't get up right away after waking up. Instead, I stared at the ceiling of the cave I had been staying in, wondering if everything I had undertaken was for not. I had been walking the ceaseless desert for days and I still had no shred of belief that something was nearby. The number of tanks I had left would be enough to get me back to the meeting place that Katya and I had discussed prior to my departure. There I could replenish my stock of oxygen and press forward once more. I found myself thinking back to the days when Kash was still alive. How the world just seemed less dreary with his presence. I hoped that Valian and Katya were doing okay in the old den of mystery. Knowing Katya, she'd spill everything they found, if anything at all.

    I managed to pull myself from the unseasonably cool ground and brush off the sand particulates that clung themselves to my clothes like a strip of velcro. I had been dreading another day with the blazing inferno raging in the sky. The desert temperatures were getting to me I think. I still had plenty of water to tie me over until I could re-stock. I stepped outside and with a defeated sigh, turned my journey homeward. As I crested one of the dunes I had traversed before, I noticed something off in the distance. A drove of... something. They were moving in an odd manner and they dotted the horizon in both directions as far as I could see. I couldn't quite make out what they were. I set my pack down, along with my oxygen tank, and procured a pair of binoculars. As I brought them to my eyes, my heart immediately sank as budding fear began welling up within me. The legion I was seeing was an army of DRAIDA scorpid guardians. The same ones that killed Kash back at our new bunker. The beaming sunlight reflected off of the machines' hard steel. This time there were hundreds if not thousands of them.

This was bad. I didn't have enough oxygen to attempt to go around the horde. It was apparent I had two choices...

Head back to rendezvous and likely suffer the same fate as Kash

or

Press forward with my remaining oxygen in one final attempt to locate a place with more oxygen.

The latter option could leave me dead due to asphyxiation, but it seemed a hell of a lot better than being torn to shreds by merciless machines.

I walked back towards my temporary camp, then set my sights past it into the continuing desert. I wiped a bead of sweat from my brow as it slowly tickled toward my eye.

"No time like the present", I told myself as I pressed forward into perilous uncertainty.

Katya Malikov- 25

We were nearing the rendezvous site. Valian tapped on his knee as he drove.

"Nervous tick, or do you have music playing in that big empty head of yours?", I jested.

"Eh, a little bit of both I think", he responded now looking down at his finger. The tapping stopped as he returned his attention to the sandy path before us. I had been shaking since we left Bios- Alpha. What was I supposed to say to Zephyr? I had so much built up inside, that I was afraid I could say too much all at once.

I guess Valian had taken notice of my internal conflict, as I felt him place his hand on mine. I looked up at him, but he did not return the sentiment. I interlaced my fingers into the spaces in his and let out a breath through my nose. I squeezed his hand rather tight. I was glad that he chose to come along at the last minute. I think all the secrets and mumbo-jumbo were getting to him as well.

"Almost there", I said, a trifle tremulous.
We began the ascent up the final hill towards the canyon. As we peaked, I saw them. I saw the sea of horror that stood between us and our dear friend. Thousands of them, wandering in a meticulous path. It looked as though they were scanning for something.

"Christ", I heard Valian say as he too took in the scope of the undulating mass before us.

I replayed the image of Kash over and over again in my head. Once for each scorpid that I saw. I felt the rage overtake me once again.

"Valian", I said icily. "Stop the car. Now"

"Are you crazy?! What are you planning to do? No, I won't" I immediately kicked the door open while the vehicle was still in motion. Valian brought it to a grinding halt.

"The only thing out there is death, Kat! There is nothing we can do! It took all of us just to bring down one of those things!"

"I'm not just going to sit here and abandon her! She would do the same for us!" I shouted back.

"No, she wouldn't! She would come up with a plan first. Calm and collected! This is just suicide!"

"Then stay and watch from the sidelines, asshole. I'm not leaving until we either get Zephyr... or what's left of her!"
I grabbed a machine gun from the back and began bolting towards the countless machines that stood between Zephyr and me. I heard Valian yelling behind me, but when I looked back he was running towards me with a gun as well. I stopped at the top of a sandy ridge, and Valian slumped down next to me, huffing and puffing.

"There's nothing I can say to stop you from doing this, is there?", He asked. I looked over at him and shook my head.

"Then we go together".

We began sliding down the ridge and firing. The scorpids took immediate notice as bullets deflected off their tough shells. A group of them broke away from their routine track and began barrelling towards us. We continued with suppressive fire, but none of the monsters were going down. The chilling roars they emanated made my hair stand on end, but I refused to stand down. If I died here it would be fighting for Zephyr. The horde grew ever nearer, still, I held fast. The two closest to us raised their tails and came in for the strike, I successfully evaded the attack and began shooting the machine from the side. I still couldn't penetrate its armor. Even at a point-blank range. This was an act of futility. I began running back to get some distance. As I did I heard the pained yell of Valian, who was running away, a large trail of blood following in his stead.

"VALIAN!" I shouted. As he looked to me I could see the blood pouring from the place his right arm used to be. I rushed over to him, and to my surprise, the scorpid that was pursuing him had turned tail and began moving back toward the horde it came from. Valian had fallen unconscious, nearing a group of boulders. He was in bad shape. If I didn't find a way to staunch the bleeding, he wouldn't make it all the way out here. Tears began welling in my eyes as I began sobbing, completely helpless.

"Please", I begged to anyone that would listen. "Please don't take him from me. Not him too."

Then came the blinding light, and a sound so loud it almost ruptured my eardrums. I spun around to see a catastrophic explosion, almost entirely decimating the throng of scorpid machines. I could see the after traces of where the blinding explosion came from. The angle made no sense to me as it indicated that whatever was fired came from skyward. I could hear

a loud whirring noise grow before all of my questions were answered. A large ship began phasing into existence.
An emblem reading one single word came into view.

DRAIDA

The ship made a gentle landing before its entry hatch slowly lowered revealing three people. One of them was wearing a white blouse that looked rather high-end. Her jet black hair pulled back into a tight ponytail and a gaudy necklace adorned her chest. She smiled as she addressed me.

"Well, I'll be damned. It's true", she said.

"Oh damn, I'm sorry. You're probably looking for an introduction. My name is Aya Rahnbyo, CEO of DRAIDA. You guys must have had one hell of a week."

She turned to the others on the platform with her.

"Get the man to medical right away, and get her on board and comfortable We have a lot of explaining to do"

The two men nodded, one walked over to Valian and began carrying him into the ship.

"H-hang on", I choked as I held a hand up. "I'm not going anywhere until I find-"

"Zephyr Apherius? She is just fine, and she will be for some time to come. Please, miss. I need you to board the ship."

"H-how do you know Zephyr?", I asked. The woman's name flashed in my head. Aya Rahnbyo. She was the sender of the email I had read back at Bios- Alpha.

"You!" I shouted. "You're the one who proposed 'Glass Shadow'! You're... you're a monster!"

I held my gun up to her. She slowly put her arms up

"I can't understand what you must be feeling right now, and I'm sorry for anything you were forced to go through, but I assure you, we are not the enemy", she said with a rather confident demeanor. "You have my word", Aya continued. "Zephyr Apherius is safe and sound."

"Then where is she? Tell me!"

"Exactly where she needs to be", Aya responded.

I then felt a hard whack on my head before everything went black.

Chapter 21- Fate Realigned

???-???

"Miss Cygnus has successfully returned Mr. Ephyon home, my Seraphim", I said in a small voice. I was blissful. Glad that no harm had come to the man chosen by Daedalus to save us all. I could feel the warmth of happiness warm me to my core.

"Things always turn out as they should, child", Seraphim said back.

As the days grew into months I became more sensitive to the tides of fate. The longer I stayed with her, the further I could see into our future. As expected the road was laden with the somber cloak of despair. Yet through all the misery, I was enlightened on, I could see a future in which we could all thrive in peace. Whether or not that peace would be sustained was uncharted territory. I had not trained long enough to see what other possibilities lie ahead that could throw a proverbial wrench into the works. Seraphim pulled me from my pondering.

"The time is nearing. Their meeting is imminent now. Remain patient, dear child and we will soon be one step closer to reuniting you with your father.

I hadn't heard him be referred to as my father in quite some time. It would seem that I would soon have to explain everything to him. If the tides of fate willed it so, then I would follow their sweet winds to my destiny. I truly hoped that I would see him again soon. I missed being his little songbird. His little Ophelia.

"Now that he has been set back on his path, by Calio, we should turn our attention to the next one", Seraphim stated.

"Zephyr Apherius", I said with a hint of curiosity. I began focusing on her and saw nothing but the vast burning yellow of endless sand.
"She seems lost. She's running out of time." I said.

"She's exactly where she should be, dear child."

Through Zephyr, I could see something through the sea of sand. A structure smack- dab in the middle of the wastelands. It was... no, it couldn't be.

"This will be the first time you are seeing home in quite some time, I'm sure.", Seraphim mentioned with a small laugh.

"Um, Seraphim? Can I stop for a while? This is too much right now.", I asked.

"Of course, child. You have earned some rest."

I got up and slumped over into my bed making a tired groaning noise into the sheets. This was a difficult undertaking. I was drained, but I knew what my purpose was. I rolled over and stared at the ceiling with a now weakened smile as for the first time in months I was able to doze off and dream of better things.

Chapter 22- Connection Established

Llaric Ephyon- 35

    I had been resting in my bed for a few hours. I could hear Calio shuffling around out in the kitchen. I was overwhelmed with questions in my head. Like a blurry image swirling around refusing to reveal itself to me. I could see the area where the arrow had pierced my body was now covered with scar tissue. I was still in awe at how quickly Calio was able to heal up such a wound. I touched it gently as if to receive some sort of understanding. I heard footsteps approach my room as my door swung open. Calio stood in the doorway still looking half- annoyed.

    "Your food supply is restocked, so now you can forget about diving headlong back into that cesspool of a city. Are you able to move?", she asked.

I sat up with little strain and swung myself out of bed.

    "Yeah I should be fine, thanks"

She beckoned me out to the kitchen where I sat down and she looked at me. It felt like she was unsure where to begin, but after a couple of pensive moments, she began talking.

    "Before you left for Malvora, you were able to... see things. Talk to people that weren't here with you, right?"

I nodded in confirmation.

    "You have been chosen by Daedalus to receive the gift of foresight", she continued.

I knew where she was going with her explanation, and I wanted to hear all of it.

"That machine in your basement that Valiance so wonderfully explained to you is a transcendental amplifier. It enhances the state your mind goes into when you speak with these people you have been seeing. I have a question.", she indicated.

"Shoot" I returned.

"Who have you been in contact with?"

I racked my brain for all of the information I could on the people I met.

"Uh Kairos the dream keeper, a guy named Masis, and a crackpot named Iyatiroh, oh and you already know about Valiance. Wealth of knowledge that guy".

Calio pondered my response for a moment and smiled.

"Everything seems to be in order so far. I shall continue. These beings have also been chosen by Daedalus to aid in the oncoming calamity."

I swallowed hard as I asked her what calamity was coming. She told me that a great war beyond anyone's comprehension was coming and that transcendent beings would be needed to quell its raging fire.

"You began seeing these people after your encounters with the Umbra, yes?"

"That's about the long and short of it yeah", I replied

"The phrase 'Without Yggdrasil, we fall', something you have undoubtedly heard numerous times before... well that's your calling. Your purpose. A fate has been written for you by Wake, himself. Yggdrasil will be your greatest weapon in the oncoming war. Harness it. Master it. You still have some way to go but you are on track to the right destination, now"

"Wait so that phrase is my purpose and it has been written for me? Who is Wake?"

"Wake is the head and founder of Daedalus. Daedalus is a society of people who are much like you Llaric. People who have seen into other worlds. Other realities... and other futures. We control the tides of fate so that we may avoid the crisis knocking at our door"

"And what could I possibly do in this 'oncoming war'? I'm just one man. One mortal man."

"You are much more than a mortal man, old friend. The things you are destined to do... no one else can do them. The war I speak of isn't just a threat to this planet or even this galaxy. This war is a threat to the very fabric of existence itself. It's everyone's problem, and everyone has their role to play. Keep on the right path. Make contact with the others you were meant to. You don't have to say anything right now, but remember this concerns you... and your daughter."

"Wait. Ophelia? She's alive?"

"Of course she is dumb- dumb. She is completely safe. Trust that everything is fine and know that with your help, Daedalus can be the force that keeps the future alive for everyone."

"Where is my daughter, Calio?" I asked, slightly heated.

"I'm sorry, Llaric, It's not time to disclose that just yet. I wish I could, but at least I can assure you that no harm will come to her. She is with someone very powerful who is caring for her."

I felt the tension release in my body as I heard those words. I couldn't remember a single thing about Calio, yet I felt an undying trust for the things she was telling me. If she said that I had to continue my work with the rifts and converse with these other beings, then that was what I was going to do. Anything to see my daughter again. Calio stood up from her chair and made her way to the door.

"I've gotta go now, but it was good to see you again. Stay on track, and keep the things I've said in mind. Goodbye, Llaric"

She cracked the front door open and spoke once more

"When you meet Soko, tell her I say hi, okay?"

"Yeah", I said flatly, "No problem"

She disappeared behind the open door and with a loud click, she was gone. I had so much to do. I had no idea how far I'd have to go, but no limit was too great. I had just received the greatest news I had heard in a long time. My little songbird was still alive and well.
"I'll do whatever it takes," I told myself. "I will not fail you again."

Zephyr Apherius- 24

The setting sun tore at my skin like a hot metal blade. I had run out of water and my lips were going numb. I was down to my last tank of oxygen. Most people I knew would be panicked by the thought of death being close enough to touch, but me? I was hoping for the safety of my friends. Praying that they didn't charge headlong into those scorpids for my sake. I hadn't given up hope yet. I was approaching a lone-standing structure in the middle of the desert. I had no idea if it was real or a mirage, but there was a chance I could find oxygen there. Or even better, an anchor. I dragged my feet through the sand, which felt as though it were purposely attempting to hinder my survival. Every step I took felt like I had a hundred pounds of lead strapped to my legs. closer. Closer. Closer it grew until I heard something. A sweet soft voice beckoning me away. As I listened in, I realized it was the voice of a child. My curiosity had piqued. What was a kid doing by themselves all the way out here? They could be in danger. I looked for the source of the voice and as it grew louder I could see a strange obelisk quite near the structure I was heading towards. As I neared it I saw that it was a sleek, jet-black mirror and on the other side of the glass was a child. She stared at me. I was confused but ran over to see if I could help her. I ran and slid to its base and placed my hand on the glass

"It's okay sweetie, I'm gonna get you out okay?"
The little girl seemed frightened as she stared into my eyes. Then she spoke.

"Hurry, he's coming"

"Wh- who's coming, sweetheart? Are you okay"
From beyond the mirror, I heard the ungodly scream of what sounded like a creature out of hell itself. Another voice invaded my head. This one was familiar to me and stopped me in my tracks.

"Don't let it fool you", the voice said within the confines of my mind

"-dad?", I said out loud. I looked up at the little girl and everything made sense. I could see the lumbering creature behind her. The same rotting corpse that plagues my nightmares. The Umbra. The little girl was.... me. I shouted at the top of my lungs at the mirror.

"YOU WILL NOT TAKE ME"

The little girl within immediately stopped crying and gazed up at me with a smile before saying her last words

"You're a good girl, you'll save us all"

With those words, the mirror exploded into millions of fine particles before being completely erased from existence. I had no idea what I had just seen, but I was sure that it was a sign that I was close to my goal. This structure... this pod-like structure had to offer some reprieve.

I had grown so tired. I was close enough now, that I could see movement inside. A man sitting down at his kitchen table. This was it. He would have something in there that would keep me alive. Now I just had to go in and take it. I pulled out a pistol with labored breaths as I ascended the stairs to the front door. I took one long breath before kicking in the door as hard as I could. I stumbled in, my vision blurring. I saw the man at the table. He seemed unphased by my forced entry. I couldn't see his face, but in front of him was an anchor, glowing in a brilliant white light. I pointed my gun at his head. The light emanating from the plant slowly began to fade as the man calmly turned to me. I couldn't believe my eyes. Sitting before me was the man who had long been invading my dreams. The man that slowly overtook the memory of my father. It was Llaric Ephyon, in the flesh. He smiled at me before speaking.

"You're not going to shoot me after we've only just met, are you... Zephyr Apherius?"

THE END

Manufactured by Amazon.ca
Acheson, AB